NO
$.I.N.

Mary Ellen Humphrey

LYNXFIELD PUBLISHING

©2013 & 2021

By Mary Ellen Humphrey

All rights reserved.

ISBN-13: 978-1441426468

ISBN-10: 1441426469

Library of Congress Control Number: 2021920572

Published by:

LYNXFIELD PUBLISHING

Revised & republished in 2021

Chapter 1

Victoria cheeked the shotgun, steadied her hand, and locked onto her target. Orpine was unaware that he was in her sights. She squinted her eyes, lifted her head for a second, smiled and thought, *I win!*

The golden retriever, Delight, spotted her and joyfully ran towards her, barking and wagging her tail. She tried to wave the dog away, but by the time Victoria recheeked her gun to aim, but it was too late. Orpine hid behind a large old fir tree.

Victoria kept the sight on the tree, despite the intense ache in her arms.

She yelled, "I know you're in there. Come out. I've got you and you can't get away."

There was no answer. "Orpine, I promise I won't shoot. Just come out. It's over-I win."

Where has that dog gone? She thought, *she's too quiet.* She grimaced. Treetops swayed in a gentle breeze and she saw in her peripheral vision shadows dancing around the pine tree where he was hiding. "You can't escape," she called hopefully. *Darn! He isn't going to make this easy.*

A branch broke behind her. "Here, girl," she called to the dog. "Come here, Delight, and stay out of trouble." She patted her leg to gesture to the dog, all the while holding the shotgun with her left hand, keeping it trained towards the pine tree.

Another branch cracked behind her, snapping too loudly to be Delight. Victoria turned, realizing too late that it wasn't the dog. Orpine had her in his sights.

"You were behind that tree," she said glancing back. "How did you get here? I watched the whole time and there was no way for you to get out."

"There was one direction you couldn't see, behind the tree."

"Delight!" he called, "Come!"

The dog ran from behind the tree where she'd been all the time and sat down near him.

"Good dog," he said, patting her head.

"Why does she mind you so well?" Victoria muttered. "She knows who's boss," he said.

"She knows who feeds her," she said, knowing full well that wasn't the complete reason Delight obeyed him but not her. The dog simply minded him and generally ignored her. Perhaps she did know who was boss.

"Maybe it's pack mentality," he teased.

"Are you saying I'm lower in the dominance hierarchy than that dog?"

"Evidently Delight thinks so."

"Victoria lowered her shotgun down beside her. "Okay, you win. I give up. Let's go home now."

"Not so quick. The pursuit isn't over yet. It's just beginning."

Orpine led her back to the log cabin despite her protests, and then tied her hands behind her. "Sit here."

"I've had enough war games for today. Come on. You won."

"The game isn't over yet because you haven't learned any new survival skills. That's the whole purpose of this," he said.

She sighed. Yerba, their cat, sunned herself on the windowsill, oblivious to any war game. *She's got the right idea*, Victoria thought.

"Orpine, untie me. I'm tired. Let's stop for now. We can finish this later."

"Trust me, dear. This is important. We have to be ready."

"I should have shot you when I had you in my sights," she said.

"Yes, that's exactly what you should have done. But you didn't. Now you have to learn your lesson. You will have to suffer the consequences for your hesitation. That will be today's lesson."

"Well, at least untie me."

"Wouldn't seem real if I did that. Round two starts in ten minutes," he said. "You should plan your next strategy while you wait." He turned to look for something in a drawer, humming a tune.

Victoria glanced at the door to the log cabin, her potential escape route. If only she could untie the ropes binding her wrists. He really tied these ropes tight. She struggled to untie them behind her keeping her eye on Orpine, her captor. Her dark hair was French braided into a long trail down to her waist, loose curls wisped around her face, and small beads of moisture formed on her brow.

Orpine turned aside for a moment to examine his weapon, an AKC assault style rifle. His shaggy brown- gray hair curled along the collar of his faded blue denim jacket and worn army boots were snugly laced over his equally worn blue jeans.

I wish he'd stop, Victoria thought, *He looks tired, too*. She noticed how gray his hair had gotten and wondered why she hadn't noticed before, and how drawn his faced seemed, at least from this view. *He looks so old for someone only forty-one*, she thought. It was a little dim inside the cottage and she hoped it was only the poor light that made him look old.

The interior of the log cabin was one large room. A kitchen area to the right and a combined living and sleeping area to the left made up the whole building. It was cozy and neatly organized except for a small desk behind her. On the desk was a compact computer and short-wave radio. She realized that he hadn't used the radio much lately, a thought that passed quickly, almost without notice.

Next to the desk was a worn guitar case. Crumpled papers littered the area around the floor near the small trashcan. They were her papers, which she had crumpled into balls and shot towards the basket unsuccessfully-her poems not composed to her liking. He'd never leave litter like that. He was too neat.

Victoria grinned remembering she'd left them there just to tease him. Of course he knew that. It was another little game, to let him know she didn't always conform to his way—a game lovers play—especially when they're all alone for long periods of time.

She didn't realize that behind her a dried, brown-stained coffee cup with a chewed pen sticking out was about to fall over the edge of the desk she was accidentally hitting as she worked to free herself. The cup teetered and fell to the floor with a crash.

"What are you doing?" he bellowed, turning around. "It's not time yet." He finger-combed his scraggly graying beard as his dark blue eyes sparkled with anticipation. Delight whined and licked his hand.

"Sit!" he commanded and the dog obeyed.

Victoria frowned at the dog and rolled her eyes mockingly. "Let me go!"

He watched her, silently, deep in thought.

Victoria squinted her eyes at him defiantly and detected a slight grin on his face. *He enjoys this*, she thought.

His watch alarm beeped. "Now it's time," he said, and loosened the ropes, taking her by the arm.

"Ouch! You're hurting me," she protested, pulling away, trying to make it difficult for him.

"You've got five minutes," he said, looking at his watch.

"Five minutes?"

He nodded outside the open door. She looked at him. He pressed her tightly against the doorjamb for a moment and looked into her eyes. "You know what's going to happen when I catch you," he whispered, grinning.

She gulped, and squirmed to get away, but he held her tight. She reached around him with her free hand and lightly unsnapped the leather holster on his hunting knife secured at this waist and slipped the knife out. She pulled her arm back behind her, holding his gaze.

"You have to catch me first," she whispered back.

He smirked and released her. Holding the dog by the collar with his left hand, he said, "I'm giving you a sporting chance. When the five minutes are up, I'll fire one shot so you'll know I'm coming."

She glanced outside doubtfully, then back at him. "Four minutes, fifty-nine seconds...." he said.

She sprinted out the door, not looking back and ran directly towards the woods about fifty feet from the remote clearing around the cottage. She ran as fast as she could down a worn path through the thick trees, pausing to look about and secure the knife in her own belt, on the side so it wouldn't cut her. She bit her lip.

If she went right, there were lots of hiding places in the hilly terrain, but she didn't want to do that because Delight would sniff her out in no time, and she'd be trapped.

She headed left into the thick woods and soon reached a stream. Then she heard the gun shot. He was coming!

She waded into the stream. The cold water was knee deep and instantly numbed her ankles. The water was always cold, running down from the nearby mountains. The warmest temperature it ever got here in the Maine Allagash wouldn't begin to heat up this water.

The rocks were slimy with green moss and she slipped in her haste, mercilessly scraping and bruising her knees and shins, even though she wore jeans. Undaunted and determined to win, she hurried down the stream about a hundred yards and exited on the opposite side, scrambling up the embankment as her feet slipped on the moss. She heard the dog barking in the distance and looked back towards the woods. *Oh no! I've got to hurry!*

10

She pulled her faded blue denim jacket off and quickly removed her shirt, placing it on the bank of the stream, hidden in some tall grass. She placed a rock on it. Her plan was to stop the dog for a few minutes, while she backtracked and ran further down the stream. As she ran, she put her jacket back on.

She climbed out the other side of the stream and nearly tripped over a lumbering muskrat. Victoria and muskrat were equally startled. She caught her breath, waited a few seconds for muskrat to scurry out of the way, and then headed back through the woods in the direction of the cabin.

Victoria stopped for a moment, gasping for air, and looked around, evaluating her situation. She heard Delight barking. *They're getting closer!*

She detoured, knowing she needed more time, and climbed up a steep incline. A tree hovered over the edge of a small cliff. She climbed up the tree, out onto one of its branches, steadying herself. The tree bent over, swaying, so she made it swing more until she could jump down to another tree, monkey-style. It took three tries until she finally grabbed the next tree and climbed down. She hurried in another direction. See if you can follow that trail, she thought.

Further into the woods, she removed a boot and a sock. She slipped the boot back on without tying it and pulled a young sapling down. She took the knife and cut a long reed of grass to secure the sock, and let it go. The sapling hung down just low enough so the dog could smell it but have trouble reaching for it.

She imagined the dog jumping up at it and smiled. Then she retraced her steps until she came to another trail and headed back in the direction of the cabin. As she ran through the woods, she keenly watched for any sign of her pursuer. Delight barked and sounded further away than before, so she was confident she had time.

When she turned onto the main trail to the cabin, she glanced back again, this time tripping on a broken branch over the trail and fell headlong. Sprawled out, she lay there, stunned for a moment.

"Oh," she whimpered. "I hope I didn't break anything." She mentally inventoried her body and concluded nothing was broken. "You and your survival games," she muttered.

Slowly, she stood up. It was very quiet. Too quiet. There was no sound of her pursuer. Her heart quickened and she scurried as quietly as she could through the woods, pushing branches out of her face as she listened for the dog. When Delight barked excitedly, she figured they had just caught up to her hidden shirt in the grass along the stream and were just realizing her trick.

They had.

She looked back for a second, smiling that she still had time for her strategy. When she looked ahead a spider web locked onto her face.

"Ugh!" She shook her head and spit it out of her mouth, batting the web off her face and rubbing her hands on her pants. She hated spiders.

The woods cleared up ahead and Victoria stopped to survey the area. There was the cabin. No one appeared nearby. She took a deep breath, then sprinted towards the front door and darted inside.

Her bootlace dragged on the floor with a mouse-like scratching sound, but she ignored it. She looked around and grabbed a rifle off the wall rack and checked the chamber, all the while glancing nervously at the doorway.

The chamber was empty. She fumbled in the drawers and found a cartridge. She clumsily loaded it into the weapon. Victoria crouched back near the bed, braced against the wall and waited, aiming the gun straight-ahead at the door. *This time I will shoot. I'm ready for you. Come and get me!*

Fifteen minutes of extreme quiet passed. Victoria thought even the wind had stopped, and the birds were gone. Her heart pounded as she strained to listen for any sign of them approaching. *Where is he?* Her arm ached from her prone position.

The dog suddenly clawed and whined at the door. Victoria stiffened and cocked her weapon. Curtains covered the windows so he couldn't see inside, but she knew he would deduce her presence because of the dog. There was only one door and she was aiming right at it. Her heartbeat increased and her palms sweated. She concentrated, trying to breathe slowly, waiting for his next move.

But Orpine didn't come to the door. She listened. There were no footsteps and Delight was now quiet. *What's he up to?*

Very slowly, with a rusty creak, the door began to open a few inches. Victoria watched, anticipating her shot as the pounding of her heart echoed in her ears. Then a large black snake slithered inside and headed right towards her!

She screamed. The door flew wide open and Orpine ran inside. Delight barked and jumped on the snake.

Orpine stopped when he saw the gun pointed at him. He grinned slightly; his eyes sparkled. With a confident sniff, he took a step towards her.

"I'll shoot! Stay right there and put down your weapon."

"You're not going to shoot me," he said. He did stop his approach.

"Yes, I will. Don't come any closer or I'll shoot." She felt her knees shake, but clenched her jaw with determination. "You have to agree now, Orpine. I win."

The snake was still slithering and the dog was biting at it. She watched it from the corner of her eye.

Orpine watched the dog and snake, too, waiting for the right moment, then, in an instant, he lunged towards Victoria and pushed the muzzle of the rifle away. He pinned her against the wall and held her arms firmly. "I've got you now!"

She glared at him. "Really?" She struggled, then stopped. "Okay, Orpine. You win." She looked him in the eye.

He stepped back with a smile, but Victoria reached behind her back and pulled out the knife. "Ha!" she said,

"Pretty good, Victoria. What are you going to do with that knife?"

"Come on, Orpine. I win. Admit it. I beat you at your own game."

He raised his hands in surrender.

She smiled and put the knife on the desk. Orpine grabbed her. "I've got you now," he said, holding her in his arms.

"And just what are you going to do to me?" she asked coyly.

He pulled her over to the bed and kissed her hard on the lips.

"No, stop!" she feigned, but he didn't.

Victoria looked over at Orpine who was sound asleep. She slid silently out of the bed, gathering a small blanket around her. She walked as quietly as she could, slowly approaching the rifle still on the floor. She grimaced as she stepped over the dead snake. Delight looked up at her and whined softly. "Shhhh," she mouthed with her finger on her lips.

The wide wooden boards of the cabin floor creaked. She cringed, stopped, and glanced back over her shoulder. He was still asleep.

She reached down and picked up the weapon. "What do you think you're doing?" Orpine demanded. Startled, she turned around. He was pointing his gun directly at her. She instantly dropped the rifle onto the floor.

"Okay. I give up. You win." She held up her hands.

He cocked his gun.

"Don't shoot. Come on, Orpine. I'm sorry, I give up. You win. Don't shoot!"

He began to squeeze the trigger.

Her eyes grew wide. "Please, don't!"

He shot. Red fluid gushed over her chest. She looked down. "You bastard! Why did you have to shoot? Look at me! What a mess."

He smiled. "Just wanted you to understand what a real-life situation would be like."

"Damn you, Orpine! You and your stupid war games! I said you win. You didn't have to shoot me. I never shoot you, and you always shoot me."

"That's just the point. You should have shot me."

"Don't you know it hurts?"

"It's just a sting. It'll go away soon, and the paint washes off. Here, let me help you."

"Stay away from me....JERK! One of these days, I'll be the one who shoots you. You'll see how it stings. Just wait until next time-I won't hesitate to shoot. Just wait!"

She pushed him aside and grabbed a towel, tossing her head so the long braid whipped by him. The dog followed her outside where she washed in a sun shower stall.

Orpine stood politely outside her stall.

"I'm not speaking to you," she said when she came out wrapped in her towel.

He handed her some daisies. "Truce?"

She pushed by him. It would take more than flowers to appease her this time. He followed her, but she slammed the cabin door in his face.

"Come on, Victoria," he called through the door. "I'm sorry. I shouldn't have shot you. I won't do it again. I promise." He reached to open the door just as the lock latched with a deliberate click.

16

He sat down on the steps with Delight beside him. "Looks like we're both in the doghouse tonight."

Delight whined and put her head on his lap.

Orpine stroked her ears lovingly. "Don't worry, girl. She can't stay in there forever."

Inside the cabin, Victoria dressed and dried her hair with her towel. She sat down to brush it out and re-braid it. There was a framed photograph on the small table next to the bed, and a colorful rag doll sitting beside it. She sat down and picked up the doll, hugging it affectionately. A single tear rolled down her cheek.

When she'd finished her braid and tied it off with a clip, she reached for the photograph and studied it as if seeing it for the first time. She touched the picture lovingly, tenderly stroking the little girl who sat on her lap in the photo. Both were dressed in matching mother-daughter outfits of red, white, and blue for the 4th of July, eight years ago. She sighed. *Had so much time passed? Time certainly didn't heal my pain*, she thought. *It's still unbearable.*

The child's hair in the photo was full of curls framing her smiling face. Victoria's hair in the photo was shorter then, but still long and wavy. She hadn't cut it since her child died. For a tortured moment she relived that awful nightmare. She saw the angry faces of her neighbors picketing the municipal building with signs, demanding they tell the truth and stop the pollution.

Victoria shook her head and held her face in her hands. "I didn't believe them," she sobbed, remembering the traffic jams as reporters besieged the place, and gawking sightseers who came into town hoping to catch a glimpse of some twisted freak of nature.

She remembered saying good-bye to each of her friends and neighbors as they moved away, one by one, until only she and a few others remained. She'd been so sure they were all over-reacting, so sure the government reports were honest and accurate, so sure there was no real danger. *It's amazing what you can convince yourself is true*, she thought, *when you really want to believe it.*

She looked at the photo affectionately. "I'm so sorry, Baby. I didn't know. Mommy is so sorry."

Victoria took her private moment to grieve for Colleen, as she so often needed to do. She knew this routine well, and she knew she would recover and go on in a few more minutes. Recover for a little while, at least, until her next grief attack. There was no survival game that could save her from this torture. People said the pain would eventually go away and would ease with time. She was certain it would not. It could not.

At least out here in the wilderness there were no honking drivers, no busy crowds to remind her, and no children she ached to hold. To that extent at least, she was safe in this self-imposed prison. Despite Orpine's war games.

Victoria wiped away her tears and put the photograph back on the table. She placed Colleen's rag doll back in its place completing her miniature shrine to her lost child. With a final sniff, she wiped her nose and turned around.

Victoria picked up the dead snake and opened a window and tossed it outside. She slammed the window shut.

Orpine looked doubtfully at Delight. "I think she's really mad this time."

Orpine sat on the steps with Delight, enjoying the warm sun on his face. He started to sing quite loudly, "Have I told you lately that I love you?"

He smiled at the dog and continued his song. Even without his guitar, he was right on tune.

Victoria smiled a little and stopped to listen. *I wonder if he's really as good a singer as he sounds, or if it's just that I haven't heard any real music for so long, it seems good?* It didn't matter because his songs always made her smile. That's what she fell in love with-his ability to make her smile despite the pain she felt inside.

He had his own pain, she knew that. His songs were from a time long ago, before all the changes and before that awful war. Before Recurring Infectious Toxemia Syndrome (R.I.T.S.). They said we lost over 250,000 soldiers, some say it was planned that way, to weaken the United States and force a new world order.

Victoria figured it was just bad decisions by bad politicians-nothing conspiratorial about it. Just incompetence. The government makes mistakes all the time. Mistakes. That's all, mistakes, that ruin people's lives. History would tell, but until then, people could believe whatever they wanted.

Most of their friends chose to believe it was some giant conspiracy. All she knew was that only five from Orpine's unit ever returned from that war, and three of them died from R.I.T.S. before Trioxin was developed.

Thank goodness Orpine and David didn't come down with the symptoms sooner. They'd be dead, too. This man who serenaded her and made her smile, he would be dead now. She glanced towards the door.

Victoria opened the door behind Orpine and put his guitar case next to him. She shut the door. Orpine grinned at the dog.

Victoria waited long enough for Orpine to be repentant and her own emotions to subside. Perhaps she had over-reacted a bit. She went outside and handed him a cup of coffee and sat down next to him on the step.

"Truce?" he asked.

"Truce," she answered, leaning with her head on his shoulder.

Delight put her head on Victoria's lap affectionately, nudging her hand with her nose.

"I forgive you, too," she said, laughing.

Chapter 2

The Wilderness Store

Orpine put his arm around Victoria and pulled her close. "You know how much I love you," he whispered.

She sighed. "Almost as much as I love you," she said, thinking, *why else would I put up with this survivalist stuff?* "

It did hurt, Orpine."

"I promise not to shoot again. It just makes the whole thing more real. Time is getting short and you need to be prepared. You need to be ready."

She sighed again but didn't say anything.

"Besides, you should have shot me. That's what I wanted you to do. When you saw me come through the door, you should have shot without hesitation. Next time, I want you to shoot. When the time comes, I want to know that you'll escape and that you won't hesitate to shoot if that's what the situation calls for. That's why I shot, Victoria, so you'd get a sense of a real situation. When you're in a war, you can't be timid. The gun will go off. You have to shoot first."

Victoria frowned. "Okay. Okay."

They sat on the steps silently for a moment.

"You were too predictable," Orpine said.

"What do you mean? I thought I did pretty well this time."

He shook his head. "I knew you were going to go that way."

"Down the stream? How did you know that?"

"Easy. You never go where there's spiders or snakes. If you'd hidden in one of those caves, you'd have had a better chance."

"Spiders and snakes!" Victoria shuddered.

"Thanks for bringing that snake into the house. That really wasn't fair!"

"All's fair in love and war. Besides, it was just a harmless garter snake. It was more afraid of you than you were of it."

"I doubt that," she said.

"It is going to be war, Victoria. Do you think they're going to play fair?"

She groaned impatiently. "Really, Orpine. I think I did pretty well, and sent you two on a wild goose chase, too. How about that?"

"I have to admit that was clever. Sock in the tree, backtracking. You're definitely learning. I must be a good instructor."

"You never anticipated that I'd get back to the cabin and find the rifle, did you?"

He nodded. "Pretty smart, for sure. But you should have climbed out one of the back windows and taken me by surprise. Now that would have been even better!"

"What about Delight? I considered doing just that, but she'd have given me away for sure. That dog would have led you right to me if I'd hidden in one of those caves, too."

Orpine pulled the dog to him. "You'll have to kill the dog."

"What? Are you crazy! No way!"

"Victoria, your life is more valuable than a dog. You are correct you know; she'd have given you away. You'll have to kill her, quietly, when the time comes. Here, you can use this." He removed a gray plastic knife out of his pocket and handed it to her.

"Keep it. It's a special plastic that can't be discovered by a metal detector. You never know when it'll come in handy."

This was too much for Victoria. She held up her hands in protest, then covered her ears and shook her head. "No! No! I don't want to hear this stuff. I don't want to talk about this anymore. I'm not going to kill Delight. I'm not going to kill anyone. This is crazy!"

He put his arm around her. "I'm only concerned about you."

He handed her the plastic knife. "Here. At least take this. Keep it with you. Someday it might come in handy."

"Let's not discuss this anymore now," she said, putting the gray plastic knife in her jacket pocket, noticing a tear in the bottom, and vaguely making a mental note to mend it later.

She leaned back, pulling away from Orpine and looked out into the forest that surrounded their remote cottage. She went along with his war games but did not share his paranoia about the authorities coming after them.

She wished he would realize that people had been believing in conspiracy theories and world government take-overs since the turn of the century. It was common knowledge to reasonable people and she didn't like linking herself to those fringe elements.

It was different for her and Orpine. They weren't doing anything wrong. They weren't criminals. She was certain of that. They just wanted to escape, him from a world of war; and her from a world of grief.

Why would anyone come after them? The paper companies had long ago abandoned these Maine woods, and besides, they had a legitimate lifetime lease. Their cabin wasn't even in an organized township. *Who could possibly want to pursue them? Why? It just didn't make any sense to her.*

Squirrels chased one another noisily in the background and Victoria and Orpine watched them while they finished their coffee. Delight occasionally looked up at the squirrels and whined. She'd had enough chasing for one day and found their playful chatter disturbing.

"It's getting chilly," Victoria said.

"Let's go inside." Orpine stood up and reached for her hand to help her up. She smiled. *It's impossible to stay mad at you*, she thought, *at least not for very long.*

Victoria began working in the kitchen. After examining items under the kitchen counter, she asked, "When are we going for supplies?"

Orpine didn't answer so she looked at him. He was sitting at the table and suddenly she noticed how tired and worn he seemed. Too tired to be caused by their afternoon games. "Are you all right?" she asked.

He nodded.

"I'll get your medicine," she said, heading for a cabinet on the other side of the cabin. When she opened the bottle, she was surprised to find it was nearly empty. Only three pills remained. "Is this all the Trioxin you have left?"

"Yes."

She looked at him, puzzled and alarmed. "Why haven't we gone to get more before now?"

"We'll go tomorrow," he said.

"Have you been taking the prescribed dosage?" She studied the bottle.

He didn't answer.

She glanced at his short-wave radio realizing he hadn't used it for nearly two weeks. She hadn't paid much attention before, but now wondered why he wasn't talking with his comrades-the others who also chose a wilderness life. It had always been a daily ritual for him. He hadn't offered any explanation for this lapse. *Maybe he really isn't feeling well. Maybe the R.I.T.S. has flared up and he doesn't want me to worry.*

The next day, Thursday, June 23rd, the three companions, Orpine, Victoria, and Delight headed down the path in the woods, each carrying a large backpack. Victoria included in her backpack a bottle of Dandelion wine for her friend, Judy, who'd told her how to make it last time they visited the Wilderness Store. She'd hiked several miles to gather the dandelions in a clearing, just to make the wine. Even Delight carried a pack and was accustomed to this trek, excited to travel along the familiar path. Several miles into the woods, Orpine stopped to rest.

"Can you keep going?" she asked. He was pale so she felt his forehead. "You've got a fever."

He shrugged. "Don't worry. I'll be fine once I get more Trioxin."

"How long have you been taking the reduced dose?" she asked.

He held her hand affectionately and smiled. "Don't worry so much. I'll be fine."

She wasn't so sure and watched him closely as they hiked further. After two more miles the sun was getting low in the sky. When they finally reached their destination, it was dusk. They both dropped their backpacks to the ground next to the camouflaged, well-hidden vehicle. Victoria unstrapped the dog's pack while Orpine began uncovering the all-terrain jeep.

Victoria opened the passenger side jeep door to air it out inside.

"Ick, what died in here? It stinks!"

She wrinkled her nose, brushed away the cobwebs, and rolled down all the windows. It had been many months since they'd make their last visit to the Wilderness Store.

Orpine lifted the hood and began replacing the distributor cap and other items he'd kept when they weren't using the jeep.

"Can you hold the light?" he asked.

Victoria watched him work as if she were really interested. Actually, she was thinking about their impending contact with other people. She wondered if there would be any young children.

She absent-mindedly felt the large gold locket around her neck, the one she always wore when they left the cabin. It kept Colleen close somehow.

She wondered why it always hurt so much. Why couldn't she bear to be around other people and their children without feeling so badly? Her arms ached to hold the children, but she knew that wouldn't ease her pain. It couldn't replace Colleen. All she could feel and see was her own little girl, in every child she saw.

She thought of her friend, Daria. Of all of Orpine's wilderness friends, she felt most comfortable with Daria, perhaps because they both were similarly tolerant of their husband's ideas.

I wonder how Daria is doing since the accident. I hope she and her children are getting along all right without her husband. Orpine is right about that-his friends do take care of their own. She suddenly felt anxious to visit with Daria and excited to catch up on news.

Victoria sighed. She hoped no one would mention Colleen this time. She knew they meant well, but she hoped they wouldn't.

Orpine told her they just felt she needed to talk about it because they sensed she hadn't gotten over it yet. Victoria resented those words, even though she knew he was trying to comfort her. Everyone was trying to help, but what good did that accomplish?

She snapped the locket open to view her daughter's picture. There was a small ringlet of her child's hair. A single large tear fell down Victoria's cheek. She closed the locket and turned back to Orpine who was just finishing up. He always wanted her to observe. It was part of her survival training just in case she had to start the vehicle herself.

"How's the fuel?" she asked when they got inside.

"Half a tank. Plenty to get us there and back, too, if necessary."

He turned the ignition and the jeep sputtered and finally started.

Victoria glanced at him wondering what he meant by that last comment.

"If necessary?" she asked.

"If we can't buy more fuel," he answered.

She didn't ask more. They drove slowly down bumpy old tote roads long since abandoned by the big paper company. Branches and leaves swished by, scratching at their vehicle. It was pitch dark when they stopped.

"Let's sleep here for the night," Orpine said. "We can go the rest of the way first thing in the morning. No sense to wake Ralph and Judy at this hour."

They unfurled their sleeping bags in the back and soon slept, Delight nestled between them. At first light, they were on their way.

It was mid-morning when they drove up to the gravel parking lot, surrounded by tall pine trees. The Wilderness Store was a log cabin, with a dark brown stained exterior that blended well in the shadows of the tall pines. It would certainly be difficult to observe from the air, camouflaged as it was. Victoria knew this was part of the survivalist plan, the ability to hide from the government if needed.

"You stay here, Delight," Orpine said, putting a leash on the dog, and attaching it to the door handle of the jeep. She whined a little but sat down to wait patiently. With any luck, her master would bring her back a doggie treat to reward her and even though the routine was infrequent, the dog remembered.

"Good dog," he said, patting her affectionately before heading into the store.

Victoria smiled. *If I tried that, she'd be whining before I got halfway inside.*

Judy spotted the customers before they saw her. "Well, it's been a while since we've seen you folks," she exclaimed. "We were getting kind'a worried."

"It has been a long time. We should have come sooner," Victoria said, but wondered why Ralph hadn't contacted them by short-wave if they were worried. She glanced at Orpine but didn't ask.

"Ralph's out back," Judy said to Orpine. He headed for the back door.

Victoria noted Judy's ruggedness. For a woman, she was particularly muscular, not in an unfeminine way. She was used to lifting and moving heavy things in the business with Ralph. It was obvious that she worked hard.

Her short curly hair looked like it didn't need much effort to maintain. The salt and pepper color blended with her weathered complexion. Victoria smiled. Ralph & Judy were certainly two of a kind, a perfect match. Both of them weathered by nature, aging together like an old barn, useful, practical, built strong and sturdy. How could two people be so alike? Co-dependence. Living out here in the wilderness.

"How's Coralee?" Victoria asked. Usually she saw her working in the store alongside her mother, but looking around, she wasn't present today.

"She's out picking some blueberries." Judy said. "She likes solitude these days, you know, those tough teenage blues. You remember when you were young?"

"Ah," Victoria said. "It must be tough out here for teenagers. Not many other folks her age."

Judy nodded.

"We need supplies, especially Trioxin. Orpine is almost out."

Judy frowned. "Been tough to get these days."

Victoria felt a sharp lurch in the pit of her stomach.

The worry transferred to her face and Judy immediately detected her concern. "Don't worry. Got a shipment coming in tomorrow. We'll put Orpine at the top of the list."

"Tomorrow?"

"Yep. That's the best we can do."

"Thank you," Victoria said, feeling a rush of gratitude, almost embarrassing. She realized suddenly how dependent they were even though they thought they were so independent, living out in the wilderness.

Judy frowned again. "Gonna be downright difficult to get supplies much longer, so we heard," she said. "Especially Trioxin."

"Why?" Victoria asked, alarm again growing inside her. She knew Orpine would rather die in his wilderness than return to society again. There was no way she wanted to be left alone out

30

here. She couldn't bear that. She couldn't bear losing another one she loved.

"They're cracking down," was all Judy said.

Victoria could tell there would be no further explanation. She was supposed to understand, after all, "they" were the enemy, "they" were hostile to the wilderness dwellers and anti-society dropouts.

Victoria felt a rush of indignation and anger. "They" always made her feel that way.

She quickly turned her attention to a pretty baby outfit hanging on a rack nearby.

"Expecting?" Judy inquired.

Victoria blushed. "No. Not for me. I need a gift for Joy. We're planning to stop by and visit them on our way back home."

She knows that R.I.T.S. leaves men sterile. Why would she ask me that?

"Oh," Judy nodded.

I'm being too sensitive. Judy didn't mean to hurt my feelings. Victoria wished she could stop her inner turmoil. Harmless comments, she knew that, but she always read too much into them.

Orpine came inside with Ralph. Orpine looked worried. Ralph was a large barrel-shaped man, rugged and salty from their hard work. Victoria knew he must have explained something to Orpine, probably the difficulty in obtaining his Trioxin. Neither man offered any comment.

"You folks are welcome to eat with us, and spend the night, too, if you'd like," Ralph said. Judy nodded. It wasn't unusual to put up customers.

"We'd be happy to stay for lunch," Victoria quickly said, fearing Orpine would decline. He needed to rest, and to have some food.

"Great, meet us up at the house in an hour," Judy said.

Victoria and Orpine went back to the vehicle and unleashed Delight. They walked the dog along a nearby path. The dog romped in a stream while they sat in the sun, resting for a while. Victoria wanted to ask Orpine about the dilemma, what he was thinking, but knew it was best to let him tell her in his own time. He was peculiar that way and didn't like prodding. He would confide in her when he was ready. They respected each other that way creating no pressure.

When they approached the main cabin, they were greeted with the aroma of barbecuing meat. "I didn't realize how hungry I was," Victoria said, picking up the pace.

Delight ran ahead. A young girl was turning the steaks over on the grill and stopped to pat the dog. Coralee was slim. Her dark hair flowed straight down her back, tied by a wooden barrette in the back. She hugged the golden retriever like a long-lost friend. Victoria felt sad for the teenager. *It must be awful lonesome out here for her.*

Ralph welcomed them with a booming hello. He liked the visitors, too. Victoria wondered if they were aware how difficult it was for their daughter to live out here at a time when most teens are just finding themselves, developing social skills, and having a good time with friends.

They probably did, she decided, but didn't want to acknowledge it because there wasn't anything to do about it. Except leave, and that wasn't an option. She'd seen Coralee's sullenness growing for a long time, since she'd become a teenager. At 16, attitude is often hard to hide.

Judy handed Ralph some tall beer glasses and he filled them from a wooden keg in the corner. It was shaded from the sun and stayed quite cool, but not cold. Still, it was refreshing. Orpine and Ralph sat down while Victoria gave Judy a hand with the food.

"I can't believe all this," Victoria said. "How did you make so much in just an hour?"

There were fresh green beans, tomatoes and cucumbers in a center dish, and biscuits still steaming from the oven.

"Ain't nothing," Judy dismissed. "Just glad to have company."

"How those steaks coming?" Judy called to Coralee.

"I think they're done," she answered.

"Bring 'em on up," Judy said. "If they ain't cooked enough, we can put them back on the grill. Don't want them overcooked."

Soon they were all seated at the table on the porch. Ralph and Orpine were talking. Victoria felt a little conspicuous. "Have you seen Daria lately?" she asked.

Judy shook her head. "Don't live here no more."

"What?"

"Nope. She left shortly after her husband died. Tragic accident, you know. We all tried to help, but she weren't satisfied."

"Smart," Coralee said.

Victoria looked at Coralee. So did Judy.

"What do you mean by that?" Judy asked.

"I just think she was smart. Taking her two children back to the real world instead of living out here like uncivilized savages."

Victoria sensed Judy's embarrassment. Ralph was silent. Victoria held her breath, hoping no one said anything to make it worse.

Coralee sat silently, looking at her food that she'd barely touched. Her jaw was clenched. This was a discussion she'd had before with her parents. Suddenly, Victoria and Orpine felt like intruders.

Delight nudged Coralee with her nose. Coralee cut a small piece of meat and gave it to the dog. The silence was broken. Ralph and Orpine resumed their conversation. Judy's body loosened. Victoria breathed.

A few minutes later, Victoria caught a comment from Ralph. "You're gonna have to find another source," he was saying. "Trioxin is one of the controlled substances that they aren't going to let us have access to much longer. Might have to go back to the VA Hospital in Bangor to get it after tomorrow."

Orpine looked worried.

Ralph saw Victoria's concern. "Now, don't get all worked up there. Maybe they'll find a cure for R.I.T.S. one of these days and you won't need that Trioxin anymore."

"Don't get his hopes up," Victoria said, really meaning both their hopes.

Judy said, "It could happen. They have made some real progress, so we hear. Course that don't mean they'll share it with the likes of us. For all we know, they already have a cure."

"Mom. Really!" Coralee blurted out.

"I hear that Shaman Gay Feathers has a cure," Ralph said with a grin.

"Don't start on that!" Judy said.

Coralee sat silently. Victoria noticed the young girls' embarrassment.

"Gay Feathers? I don't think I've heard of him?" Orpine said.

"Bout 20 miles west of here. He's helped quite a few vets, so I been told. They claim they never felt better after a visit to him. You ought to give it a try. You got some time to kill before tomorrow's shipment comes in."

"Pagan savage!" Judy scorned.

"Don't knock it," Ralph said, pointing at her with his fork, as he chewed his latest bite of meat. "Several of the guys claim he's genuine. They're wives do, too." He winked at Orpine and Victoria.

"The Lord will have something to say about that," Judy said, pointing right back.

"Not saying it's a cure, mind you," Ralph says, turning to Orpine, "but they do say he helps them feel better. Some kind of herbs and potions."

"Not a Christian ritual," Judy cautioned. "I wouldn't put no stock in those rumors at all. I'm surprised at you, Ralph. You ought to know better."

Coralee got up. "I'm not hungry. Do you mind if I leave?"

There is a silent pause. Ralph nodded his head. "Go ahead. But come back to help your mother with the dishes when we're done."

"Can I take Delight for a walk?"

"Sure," Victoria answered. "Use her leash."

Girl and dog headed into the woods, dog's tail wagging eagerly. Both seemed glad to be taking a walk.

Victoria watched her walk away and suddenly it occurred to her that Colleen would be about the same age as Coralee now. She quickly changed her focus at that thought.

"So who is this Shaman Gay Feathers, Ralph?" she asked.

They finished dinner. "I'm going to go find Delight," Victoria said to Ralph, after helping Judy clear the table and wash up the dishes. "Sometimes she's a bit hard to handle. I wouldn't want Coralee to have trouble with her."

Actually, Victoria wanted to check on Coralee and see if she was all right.

She headed down the path where Coralee had gone. Ralph and Orpine were sitting on the porch, smoking cigars, and still talking. Judy went back to the store.

Coralee had gone almost a mile into the woods. Victoria was thankful the path was well worn or she might have lost her way. She was about to turn back when she heard Delight barking. Coralee was sitting against a large grey birch tree near the stream. Victoria wondered if the girl was asleep.

She approached and noticed a rolled paper in the girls' hand. Coralee woke when Victoria approached. She sat up straight, looking a little guilty, and quickly hid the butt.

"What's that?" Victoria asked, knowing the answer.

Coralee didn't answer, just looked off in the distance. Victoria wondered if she were deliberately avoiding talking to her, or still disoriented from the drug.

"Does your mother know you use this stuff?" Victoria knew the answer, but somehow the right words to avoid sounding accusatory didn't come to her.

"It's none of your business!"

"That's true," Victoria said. "I'm not trying to be nosy. This stuff isn't good for you."

"What's it gonna do to me? Make me a half-wit? Maybe I'll forget my lousy life. What's so bad about that?" Victoria was taken aback by Coralee's anger.

"It can't be all that bad," she started to say, but Coralee interrupted.

"Yeah? What do you know? I have no friends. The only people I know are nuts, like my folks. Off on some conspiracy case. At my expense!"

"You have friends, Coralee. I've seen you with them."

"Oh, sure. Once a month if I'm lucky. I can't even talk to them by radio anymore."

Victoria paused. "Radio?"

"Ever since the mandatory black out Dad won't let me use it. Claims that's how they'll find us. Some new technology that allows them to locate us dissidents by our radio transmissions. If you ask me, they're all nuts! Let them find me. I welcome it."

Victoria sat down beside her. She waited for a moment before speaking, wondering what words to use. "This stuff is bad, Coralee. It won't help."

The girl sniffed. "That's for me to decide."

"Your parents wouldn't want you to use this. How long have you been smoking?"

She didn't answer. The dog nudged the girl's hand looking for a pat. She stoked the dogs' ears.

"You gonna tell on me?"

Victoria paused. "Your parents love you. They need to help you."

"Great. Take everything away from me. In the end, they'll be no more Coralee. Is that what you want?"

"I can't not tell them. It wouldn't be right."

"You know it isn't fair, what they're doing to me. I know you do. Why would you take their side?"

"I'm not taking their side. I don't have any choice," Victoria said weakly.

Coralee stood up. "Do what you have to. I really don't care." She walked away.

Chapter 3

Feathers & Dragons

It was nearly four o'clock when they arrived at the Native American Village. When they turned a corner, out of the thick forest appeared an authentic scene, like a photo in an old history book come to life.

Teepees and huts interspersed, children running around with dogs chasing sticks, and women tending fires while cooking food. There were racks of drying meat at the far end, the aroma reaching Delight's nostrils. Victoria held the dog's leash tighter, lest she run to the tasty parcels.

Children stopped to watch the visitors. Women warily glanced from the corner of their eyes, continuing their chores.

A man came out of the center hut. He was dressed in a colorful robe, with beads embroidered in the shape of an eagle on the front. Around his neck hung a leather pouch, most likely filled with mystical herbs.

Victoria smiled. It is just as Ralph described. She hoped they were as friendly as he promised.

"Welcome," the man bellowed. "I am Stormy Gay Feathers."

The Shaman had long disheveled gray hair that looked like it had never been combed. His deep blue eyes sparked.

"I am Orpine. This is my wife, Victoria. We hope we're not intruding."

"Never intrude. Welcome to our home."

Several children came close the man, some holding onto his robe.

"Hold your dog securely. Come. Follow me. I think I know what you need."

When he turned around, beading on the back of his robe was in the shape of a moose.

Victoria glanced at Orpine wondering if he knows she was thinking, *what's with the dog?* She smiled. At least this would be an interesting change.

Inside the hut, many of the children sat down around the man. He smiled at his guests. "Meet my offspring. Here, Foxglove, say hello."

A youngster about four stepped forward and grinned at Victoria and Orpine. He eyed Delight who was much bigger than the child.

"Hello, how are you?" Orpine said.

The boy scurried back to the safety of his father.

"This is Clover. She is sweet in her disposition," Gay Feathers said. "And here is Fireweed, Sumac, Sorrel and Ivy."

"How nice," Victoria said, smiling at Orpine.

"How prolific?" Orpine said. "And who is their mother?"

The Shaman laughed. "Have many mothers!"

He pointed outside to a woman working the firepit. "That is Snap Dragon. Her children are there with her, Daisy and Dandelion."

40

Victoria wondered if the Shaman had named them intentionally after wild plants, and why. She knew he must have but wondered why anyway. Twins climbed into the man's lap. "Violet and Honeysuckle would like to know your names?"

"I am Orpine. This is my wife, Victoria."

"And this is Delight, our golden retriever," Victoria added.

"Orpine-a plant that lives forever," the Shaman said contemplatively. "Its leaves never die."

Victoria swallowed.

"Well, that's kinda why we're here," Orpine said. "I have R.I.T.S., and there are rumors that you might know how to cure it."

"Ah, yes. But you will not die. No man dies when he leaves offspring, such as these, to carry his life energy. Part of us remains in of us forever. It is a great mystery, but not so complicated."

I think he's been drinking too much of his own concoctions! Victoria thought. *Orpine has no children. It's impossible. So much for Gay Feather's mystic powers.*

The man sensed her cynicism. She saw it on his face, but he didn't seem disturbed at all by her distrust. In fact, she detected some amusement in his eyes that sparkled like stars in the night sky. *He must be a real charmer. No wonder he has so many children!*

"You two stay in special teepee tonight. Too late to go. I have gift for you-gift from the Great Spirit, Mother Earth."

"That's very kind of you," Orpine said intending to decline the offer.

41

"No. It is intended. You cannot refuse gift from Mother Earth. Feel better after that. All problems taken care of. No more worry. Trust me."

"Guess we can't argue with that," Victoria said, smiling at Orpine.

"You go with Snap Dragon. She prepare you," Gay Feathers instructed Victoria. "We take good care of your dog."

Orpine grinned. "Go ahead. I'll make sure Delight is ok."

"You, come with me," Gay Feathers said to Orpine. "Not leave you out. Have special preparation just for you."

Snap Dragon giggled all through the bath. Victoria couldn't believe how wonderful it was-the herbs in the water and the luxurious suds. She didn't even feel shy about this strange native woman who assisted her with the bath.

Snap Dragon was uncanny in her beauty, up close, her skin was golden and her dark hair shone in the late afternoon light, reflecting the red hues in the sunset.

And what was so funny? The woman giggled incessantly. Victoria smiled. She would definitely have to ask these natives which wild herbs they used. Hopefully, they grew in her neck of the woods, too.

Snap Dragon handed her a beautiful robe, brilliantly colored, and decorated with deer and rabbits. It was marvelous how talented these folks were.

Victoria was led to a teepee on the outskirts of the village and felt quite special as the natives watched her procession through the small village.

Orpine was already inside. Shaman Gay Feathers brought in a tray containing two tall drinks in wooden vessels. The wood was intricately carved with all sorts of wildlife. A small fire was lit in the middle of the teepee, and the Shaman threw some dried leaves into it. Immediately, a pungent, sweet aroma filled the teepee.

"You must drink all of this; do not leave any. Then you will see."

"But, Orpine is the one who is sick. I am fine," Victoria said. "He needs the medicine, not me."

Gay Feathers smiled. "Do as I say, and all will be well. I will come to wake you in the morning."

"Where is Delight?" Victoria asked, still worried about her dog.

"She is here, outside your door. She will wait until morning, too. She is obedient dog, not like some mangy mutts. Don't worry. Now, drink."

Orpine grinned at Victoria. "These natives sure are hospitable," he said.

"Did they give you a bath, too?" Victoria asked.

"Yes. Smells the same as yours," he laughed.

She reached for the two glasses. "Well, drink up."

"What do you think is in it?" Orpine asked, eyeing the brew suspiciously.

"Who knows? It smells good." She took a sip. "It's delicious," Victoria said after another sip. "Very good. Try it."

"Drink up," Orpine said. "Remember, we have to drink it all."

They both felt warm, inside from the drink, and outside from the bath and incense fire. Victoria looked into Orpine's eyes. It was as if she were seeing into his very soul. The emotion overwhelmed her and tears streamed down her cheeks.

Orpine touched her ever so gently. Both were feeling pure love. An unseen magnet seemed to draw them closer. Every sense was enhanced, every sensation magnified. Soon, Victoria and Orpine embraced, locked in passion unlike anything they'd ever experienced.

The room whirled, the smoke swirled, and the two rolled and moaned as sexual anxieties overcame them. They forgot anyone else was within a hundred miles. The world was theirs. It was as if all their passion was gathered and released in one night, in one marathon of love.

Delight stuck her nose inside the teepee for a moment, whined and went back outside.

"Time to wake up," Gay Feathers said, standing over their disheveled bedding. Victoria, embarrassed, pulled the blanket around her. She was still groggy from the night, and perhaps from the potion he'd given them. She was sure it didn't cure R.I.T.S., but Ralph was correct, it did make them both feel better. She could tell Orpine felt the same way by his expression.

"When you're dressed, come outside. It's time to go." With that, Gay Feathers turned and left.

Orpine laughed. Victoria laughed, too. They hugged, nestled in the blankets for one last moment. Delight came inside and nudged between them, so they got up and dressed.

44

"Thank you," Orpine said to Gay Feathers as Victoria snapped a photo of the Shaman and his many children. "How can I repay you?"

He shook his head. "You be okay now. That pay enough," he said, his dark eyes sparkling more than ever. He winked at Victoria, and she felt her face blush.

"Remind me to thank Ralph," Orpine said, once they were heading back towards the Wilderness Store.

"I don't think you should tell him about last night," Victoria said, and they both laughed. It felt so good, that heaviness lifted, even if only temporarily. *I wish this feeling could last.* Of course, she knew it wouldn't.

"Are we still going to stop and see David and Joy?"

"You bet."

Eight miles from the Wilderness store, they turned onto a little-used tote road. Soon, they were at David and Joy's tiny cabin. David spotted them first and called to Joy, who wobbled out to greet them.

She was due soon, and by the looks, could be having twins. Victoria pulled out the gift she'd purchased from the store. It was sure to come in handy, and she knew they didn't have a lot of money to buy baby clothes. She suddenly wished she'd bought more and decided to do so when they got back to the store with instructions for Judy to give them to Joy next time they were in.

Victoria gave Joy a big hug, and Orpine grabbed David with a masculine bear hug. "It's so nice to see you guys," Joy exclaimed.

Victoria knew that Joy must be anxious about the birth of their first child. Thank goodness David didn't contract R.I.T.S. If only Orpine had been transferred out at the same time as David. Then things might have been so different.

The two men headed off into the woods where David showed Orpine his new project, harnessing the stream for energy. Delight followed, wagging her tail.

Joy fixed a cold iced tea and the two women sat down for a chat in the shade of the large oak in front of the cabin.

"Tell me what you two have been up to? What brings you out our way?" Joy asked.

Victoria blushed, surprised at herself, and certainly not intending to discuss Shaman Gay Feathers.

"We needed supplies at the Wilderness Store. Orpine is nearly out of Trioxin. Are you all set for the delivery? It must be nearly time?"

"Oh, yes. The midwife is planning to come. David is going to use the short-wave for a special signal when my labor starts. It's all planned."

"Aren't you worried?   What if there are complications?" Victoria regretted her skepticism but couldn't stop the words.

"Oh, no. Not at all. The Lord promises to save the woman in childbirth if she is faithful. I have nothing to worry about."

Victoria felt a pang of apprehension, and fear for her friend, but nodded as if she understood. *She's so young,* she thought, *and naive.*

"I shouldn't say anything. I know David would want to ask Orpine himself, but we are hoping you two would be god-parents to our child?"

Victoria was stunned and smiled. "Of course. I'd be honored."

Joy beamed. "And David plans to name our child after Orpine if it's a boy."

"I don't know what to say. That's so nice. I'm sure Orpine will be pleased." She now wished even more that she'd purchased additional baby items of their friends.

Joy looked at Victoria for a moment, a serious expression coming over her face.

"What is it?" Victoria asked.

"Does Orpine still have those nightmares?"

Victoria nodded, thinking, but he didn't have any nightmares last night.

"How is David?"

"I worry about him. It's awful. Sometimes he just cries and cries. I can't imagine the horror he witnessed, and I feel so helpless. What can I do for him?"

"All you can do is love him," Victoria said, realizing that was exactly true and the only answer. There was indeed no cure for their war-ravished hearts. And like her own pain, it would never completely go away. The only ointment for a broken heart was love. Thank God, she had Orpine's love. What would she do without him?

"I just wish I could help. Maybe our child will bring him happiness," Joy said, and then realized that Victoria didn't have that option. The apology showed on her face.

47

"I know your child will bring you great love," Victoria said with a smile. "I can't wait to find out if it's a boy or a girl. By the looks of you, it could be both!"

They laughed. Victoria was not offended in any way and Joy sensed that. Deep down, Victoria wasn't disappointed when Orpine told her they couldn't have children. The only regret she had was for Orpine because he took the news so hard, but she'd felt relieved, and a little selfish because she knew he wanted children. Women could transfer R.I.T.S. to their developing fetus, but men couldn't. The problem was Trioxin made men sterile.

She didn't tell him the truth, that she couldn't bear the possibility of losing another child. She was certain that it was not for her to be a mother again. Perhaps she was punishing herself, but it made no difference. With Orpine's disease, the future was uncertain at best. No, she'd decided long ago, it was for the best.

Soon the men returned. "Did David tell you they want to name their son after you?" Victoria asked.

Orpine turned to David. He nodded with a broad smile.

"Do you know the ribbing I've endured from that name?" Orpine said with a laugh.

David put his arm around Joy. "We've already picked out a nick-name-Piney. Like all those big pine trees out back."

"And, they want us to be god-parents, too. Isn't that nice?" Victoria said.

"I'm indeed humbled, my dear friends, that you think so much of me," Orpine said solemnly.

David grinned. "Don't get all choked up on me. There aren't a whole lot of choices out here, you know."

"Are you going to be okay when the time comes for the delivery?" Victoria asked David, despite Joy's confidence.

"Well, we have everything planned, if that means a damned thing out here. The only problem is the radio because we're not supposed to use it you know. It ain't been working too well lately anyway. Guess I can assist in the delivery if I have to. Women been having babies on the earth a long time so it can't be that complicated."

Victoria wasn't assured with that response.

"Women have been dying in childbirth on this earth for a long time, too. What if Joy has complications?"

Joy looked worried but spoke up confidently. "I told you, Victoria. We're all set. I'm not worried."

"It ain't good to get an expectant mother all worked up," David said.

"I'm sorry," Victoria said.

"My radio acts up too. Lots of static sometimes," Orpine said to bridge the awkward moment.

"They're probably trying to stop us from communicating," David said.

"Check the batteries, guys! Maybe it's just a loose connection," Victoria said. *They, again!*

"I ain't worried at all. I have the Lord's promise, and with the Lord on my side, there isn't anything to worry about," Joy repeated.

"That's what I love about you, honey. You're such a brave girl," Dave said, giving her a hug.

Victoria wondered about the brave part. It could be foolish. It could be fool hearty. It could be ignorance. She hoped it was faith. But she knew all about foolish and ignorance and faith. What had it gotten her?

They said their good-byes and were soon on their way. Victoria noticed Orpine was tired. "I can drive if you want," she offered, but he declined.

She reached in back for his Trioxin and discovered it was empty. Orpine glanced at her and looked back at the road without a word. She wondered how long he'd gone without a dose. And how much longer he could go.

Chapter 4

Friday, June 24th

"What's that?" Victoria asked, looking at the dark plume in the sky up ahead. Till now, they had driven along silently since leaving David and Joy.

Orpine knew Victoria was worried about Joy. Victoria knew she was worried about Orpine, about Trioxin, about the nightmares, and she was worried about their friends having a newborn out here in the middle of the wilderness.

There was plenty to think about as they traveled along. The smoke brought reality back into focus.

"I hope it's not a forest fire," Orpine said, frowning. They hurried forward, both aware that as they neared their destination, the plume of smoke was coming from the same direction. The air was heavy with ash. Victoria rubbed her eyes and rolled up her window.

When they turned onto the driveway to the parking lot of the Wilderness Store, they sat stunned. The scene before them was surreal. The whole store including Ralph and Judy's home behind it was burned to the ground. Black timbers still smoldered and dark smoke rose from the hulks that so recently were buildings.

"My God! What happened?" Victoria asked, breaking the silence.

Orpine looked around nervously, then backed up and hurried down the road. "We gotta get out of here!"

"Orpine. Slow down!" Victoria held onto the door to steady herself as they bumped over the rough road. She feared the bumps might do damage to the vehicle. *Why doesn't Orpine realize that, she wondered?*

Delight whined from the back seat, unable to steady herself, tumbling around helplessly in the back.

A few minutes later, Orpine saw another vehicle parked on the side of the road ahead of them. He slowed down.

"It's Ralph," Victoria said, recognizing the man when he looked up from the engine he was repairing. Orpine parked behind the vehicle and jumped out.

"Wait here. I'll find out what's going on."

He was unshaven and shaggy, his clothes worn-looking, like he'd been in them for days. That was Ralph. He always looked that way, but today, something was different. There was a heaviness about him. His movements were slow and anguished. She wondered what had happened and where were Judy and Coralee?

Orpine greeted Ralph with a warm handshake and pat on the back. They talked, gesturing animatedly for several minutes, and then both sat down.

Victoria couldn't hear their words even when she rolled her window down and tried to listen from the jeep. Delight whined, nudging her with her nose. "Shhh...I can't hear...It's all right, girl. Shhh..."

Both men returned to the jeep carrying some boxes from Ralph's truck. They put them in the back of the jeep. Victoria looked at Orpine for an explanation.

"We're taking Ralph to Cappy and Edith's. His truck broke down. Judy is waiting for him there."

Ralph climbed in back with Delight. He nodded a somber greeting to Victoria.

Cappy and Edith, Victoria frowned. *Great! My two most favorite people!* She remembered the last time they'd visited these people. It had been the worse fight she and Orpine ever had, arguing over Cappy and Edith. She didn't want a repeat.

"What happened to the Wilderness Store?" she asked.

"They did it." Orpine answered in a detached manner.

"They? Who are they? What did they do?" Victoria flushed with anger and impatience, as if everyone understood something important except her. Mixed with her anger was panic. *What if everyone had been right all along? What if they really were the enemy?*

Ralph leaned forward and stated bluntly. "The authorities burnt down my place. Came after you left yesterday. Three black helicopters. We just barely got out, thanks to a warning from some friends on the short wave who told us they were coming. Weren't no reasoning with them. They just burnt it down right in front of us."

Victoria heard defeat in Ralph's voice. She stared at him. "Why?"

"Cause we don't conform to the rules is why," he answered impatiently.

Judy hurried outside when they drove up to the log cabin. Her faded jeans were not particularly flattering to her broad hips and rugged thighs. Her blue plaid woolen jacket was worn but looked comfortable. Victoria knew these weren't Judy's own clothes and must be borrowed from Edith.

Judy hugged Ralph tearfully. "I was so worried about you."

"I'm okay," he said, embarrassed. "Look, Orpine and Victoria came along just in time to give me a lift after my truck broke down. How's that? See, my luck is changing already." He laughed, but Judy didn't smile.

"Any sign of Coralee?" she asked.

Ralph shook his head. "I'm sure she hitched over to her friends when she saw trouble. She'll show up. Try not to worry."

Victoria remembered Coralee's hike into the woods and wondered if she'd gone to smoke dope. Surely not after her parents found out.

Judy pulled back and looked Ralph straight in the eye. "How bad is it?"

"It's bad. Everything's gone." He looked down.

"Everything?" she whispered.

He nodded. Orpine and Ralph went back to the jeep to carry his things inside.

"I'm really sorry about the Wilderness Store," Victoria said to Judy.

Judy nodded. "I was afraid something like this would happen. It was just a matter of time. Ralph wouldn't listen. He can be so stubborn sometimes. I told him we needed to do things according to the rules, but he just wouldn't listen."

Victoria said, "I think I'll go help Orpine. He's not feeling too well." She didn't want to pursue the conversation further.

"What's wrong?" Judy asked.

"He's out of Trioxin."

Judy looked worried. "He's completely out?"

Victoria nodded.

Victoria preferred to head back to their own cabin, but worried that Orpine should rest, so accepted Cappy and Edith's invitation to spend the night, reluctantly.

Cappy was a short and thin man, in stark contrast to Ralph. Cappy was by no means weak since very ounce he had was muscle. His nickname fit him since he always wore a cap, even inside.

Orpine told Victoria it was to hide an old war wound, but she suspected otherwise. More likely, to hide prematurely thin hair, she figured. He always wore green camouflage. Even his cap was green.

Edith was thin and agile, dressed in forest-green denim coveralls. Her hair was short, practical, and she wore heavy woodsman boots that were always half-laced up.

Their cabin was larger than Orpine and Victoria's and had inside plumbing and extra bedrooms. They were the closest thing to a motel in the wilderness and often took in travelers.

Outside the cabin was camouflaged, too. Even the roof was made to look like evergreen trees. The large stone fireplace in the living room was a natural gathering place. After the jeep was unloaded, they all sat with a cool drink in front of it, even though the fire was unlit.

"We knew it was going to happen, sooner or later," Edith said, sitting on the arm of the chair where Cappy sat with her hand resting on his shoulder.

"It was inevitable," Cappy agreed.

"The Lord's will," Edith chirped.

Victoria could barely control her expression at Edith's comment so she looked at the unlit fireplace, studying the various stones. *What does the Lord have to do with burning down the Wilderness Store?*

"Well, I don't know how much the Lord had to do with it," Ralph stated as if he'd read Victoria's mind. "But it seems to me it was the authorities that flew those helicopters and started those fires and destroyed my store with everything in it."

"Did you get a chance to talk to anyone," Orpine asked.

"I tried. They were too busy destroying the place to listen to me. It was apparent they was set on a mission. I left quick as I could when I overheard the sergeant telling one of them to detain me."

"I'm surprised they didn't arrest you and take you away," Judy said somberly.

"I didn't hang around waiting to be taken into custody, or as they like to put it, to be violated."

"It's the End Days," Edith moaned, nodding her head.

"She's right. Ours is the last pocket of true Christianity that's left. They are going to persecute us till there aren't any of us remaining, that's their mission for sure," Cappy said.

"The Lord will reward those who are faithful," Edith advised.

Orpine glanced at Victoria knowing how she felt about some of his more fanatical religious friends. She sat silently, but he knew she wasn't pleased.

"Nothing happens without a reason," Edith said. "It's all part of a great plan."

Victoria could contain herself no longer. "That's bullshit! Lots of things happen without a reason. It's called LIFE, as in get one!"

She knew her words were overreacting to Edith, but she couldn't help herself. She'd heard all this too many times before.

"Can't change what's meant to be," Edith said. She didn't like her faith being challenged any more than Victoria liked hearing her simplistic ideology.

"Uh, what Victoria means is that we shouldn't make excuses," Orpine offered, hoping to diffuse the tension.

"I can speak for myself, Orpine. What I mean is we should take responsibility for our own decisions. God isn't to blame for everything that happens to us, good or bad. Sometimes, we just screw up!"

Edith's expression changed. It was that oh-you-re- not-a-true-believer look, excusing her disagreement. After all, she wasn't really one of them. Victoria knew what Edith was thinking, that she wasn't called, not one of the chosen, that she was lacking the Holy Spirit so therefore she was incapable of understanding her beliefs, or Truths, as Edith liked to refer to them.

Or was it sympathy? Victoria wondered was Edith dismissing her outburst because of Colleen? She felt her face grow hot. She learned long ago there was no since arguing with Edith and regretted her outburst.

"Excuse me. I need some air." She got up and headed outside. Orpine stood up to go with her, but she reached her hand out to stop him. "It's okay. I just want some time alone."

It was after noon when the men went back to fix Ralph's truck. Edith went with them.

Victoria took Delight for a long walk and when she returned, sat on the front porch with Judy, waiting for them to return. It was getting late in the afternoon.

"We better have dinner ready," Judy said as the sun got lower in the afternoon sky. These guys will be hungry when they get back."

The sun had that same pink glow as it did the night before, at the native village. Victoria remembered how good they both felt. She knew it wouldn't last. What was Gay Feathers talking about, fixing everything? Still, she was thankful for the reprieve, if ever so brief.

Victoria peeled potatoes and carrots and Judy filled a large pot with venison and vegetables. It simmered while Judy prepared her famous biscuits. Victoria set the table wondering if Edith would mind them taking over the kitchen. She decided not, since Edith was more inclined to mechanics and outside chores.

Judy had obviously spent a lot of time in this cabin and knew her way around. Victoria watched her work, impressed by her unpretentious and warm manner.

"I've got something for you," Victoria said, searching her backpack. "I almost forgot it." She pulled out a bottle. "Dandelion wine."

Judy smiled. "Let's have a glass now while we wait." She retrieved two glasses from the old pine hutch in the corner, and they sat down in front of the fireplace. It was still unlit and Victoria surmised it was because they were afraid of the smoke giving away their location. She put on a sweater.

"Don't let Edith get to you," Judy said.

"Oh, I know. I guess I'm too sensitive," Victoria said, wishing she could take back her outburst.

"She doesn't mean any harm. We've told her not to proselytize, but she can't help herself. It's not up to us to decide who believes and who doesn't."

Victoria sighed and took a big sip of her wine.

"She just gets carried away," Judy said. "Someday, you've got to tell me how you made this wine. It's delicious."

"It's your recipe," Victoria said, smiling.

"Well, you must have done something different. Mine never came out this good."

"I used lots of dandelions!"

"How is Coralee?" Victoria asked.

Judy sighed. "She's ok. Got word this afternoon that she's safe.. We're picking her up at her friend's home in a few days."

Delight barked. "They're back," Judy said, looking out the window.

"Boy, it sure smells nice in here," Cappy said when they came into the kitchen.

Orpine gave Victoria a quick hug, wondering how she was. She smiled back. "Judy's a great cook. Wait till you see what she made for dinner." He was reassured she was in a much better mood.

After everyone got seated around the large oval table, Cappy offered grace.

"Dig in," Judy said as an "amen" to his long prayer. "Before it gets cold!"

"You're going to spoil my husband," Edith said with a grin. "He's not used to such delicious cooking."

"She's right," Cappy said, winking at Judy.

"Thanks a lot," Edith teased back. "You don't seem any worse for the wear."

"Guess I'm used to your cooking by now," he kidded. Everyone laughed.

"Edith makes great meals," Judy said. "I know. I've had many here in this kitchen."

"She don't fancy things up like you do," Cappy said.

"Basics," Edith stated. "Got to keep the temple of the Lord pure. I prefer simple to fancy."

Orpine glanced at Victoria. Her smile faded with a not-again look.

"How about some of Laura's Dandelion wine?" Judy asked, glancing at Victoria for approval, undaunted by Edith's last comment.

"It'll go great with your venison stew," Victoria said.

"I'd like to make a toast," Orpine said.

Everyone looked at him expectantly. What would he say on a day with such distress?

"To freedom, and to good friends."

"Agreed," Cappy said. They all nodded.

"Freedom," Ralph sighed. "How much longer are we going to have any freedom? Things are getting worse. The government is involved in everything, much more now than when we first came here, and it was bad enough then."

"Just like the prophecies," Edith said quietly.

"The United Nations Resolution passed last month, you know. The whole world is working under a central monetary umbrella now. Only a matter of time before they take over the country," Cappy said.

"They already have," Edith stated, nodding emphatically.

Victoria shifted uneasily, chewing her food even though it suddenly didn't seem to have any flavor. Orpine was listening to his friends.

"I haven't heard any news for a while," he said. "What's going on now?"

"Didn't you hear? The new worldwide currency system is supposed to be in place by the end of the year. First they set it up here in the United States, to test it and work out all the bugs. I guess they figured if they could convert all of us, they could persuade just about everyone. After all, most of the wealth belongs in this country."

"Not anymore," Edith said, shaking her head. "They are taking our wealth and redistributing it to poor countries. We're not supposed to prosper any more than anyone else. That's part of the New World order. Steal from those that have and give to those that have not, no matter what they believe or how pagan they are or how cursed by God."

"And if we don't like it, those United Nations soldiers will invade and force it on us," Cappy stated.

"They're already here," Edith said. "Who do you think burnt down The Wilderness Store?"

"We're only supposed to have so much wealth per person, so no one is disadvantaged. Doesn't matter if you worked for it or not. Wait until those fools figure it out," Cappy said.

"What do you mean?" Victoria asked. "Fools?"

"The mainstream people back there who think this new system is just wonderful. Wait until they see all their money gone and can't get any of it back."

"You make it all sound like some grand conspiracy," Victoria said, looking at Cappy. "How could anything that grandiose be done? It defies reason. I could understand not liking some new system. Everyone feels apprehensive when changes first come along. It's always that way, but there's no way our government is going to give away all our wealth to the rest of the world. That just doesn't make sense. Why would they do that?" *They, again!*

"Socialism," Edith said. "They lost the cold war so now they're fighting us right in our own back yards and attacking the very fiber of our Christian society. And we're too stupid to know it."

"It's been a constant erosion of freedom," Cappy said.

"He's right," Ralph said. "We've been winnowing away our personal rights for years. It starts out with a new program that sounds good, might even intend to help, but ends up taking away a little more of our freedoms. Look how hard it is to own property now. Didn't used to be that way."

"We are guaranteed our freedom in the Constitution," Victoria argued. "No one can change that."

Edith laughed. "Take a look around. We are the last bastion of freedom there is in this country. We are their only hope to survive this assault. Someday, people will thank us for maintaining the free militia."

"It's our duty," Cappy said excitedly. "The history books will one day record our efforts as the few who saw through the big lie, through the conspiracy. They may call us crazy now, but they won't when it all comes to a head, and we save their asses."

"Well, I think we gain something for each freedom we give up," Victoria argued.

"Like, we may not own our property, but we don't pay high property taxes anymore."

"Bad example," Orpine said. "Everyone pays a use tax now."

"Well, what about healthcare? Before the government took over, people were left out. Now everyone has healthcare. You have to admit that's improvement."

63

"Sure, but the quality isn't as good as before," Ralph said. "I remember when I was a kid, people could choose any doctor or hospital they wanted. Now you have to go where the government says and do what their doctors tell you, whether you agree or not."

"But the point is everyone has healthcare now and no one is excluded."

There was silence.

"Look, all I'm saying is that we should be careful about believing sweeping conspiracy schemes. I just think that's dangerous. It's not healthy."

"I would think it would be easy for you to believe, after what happened to your daughter," Edith said.

"That's not fair," Victoria said. She bit her lower lip, holding back tears.

"She's right, Edith," Judy said. "Why do you need to convince people? Let Victoria believe what she wants. It doesn't change anything."

"If it's true, why hide your eyes?" Edith said defiantly.

"But that's just it, you don't know that any of this is actually true," Victoria said.

"Maybe you don't know it's true, but I do," Edith said.

"I guess I'm just not convinced," Victoria shrugged.

Cappy turned to Orpine. "You folks can have the back bedroom. Ralph and Judy got our room. We'll take the living room. It has a nice pull-out bed."

"Oh, we don't want to put you out. We have our sleeping bags," Victoria said.

"Nonsense," Ralph said. "Too late to head out tonight. You two need a good night's sleep and tomorrow will look a lot brighter. Orpine needs some rest, that's obvious for anyone to see."

Victoria had noticed it, too. Orpine was pale and drawn. His condition was deteriorating without the Trioxin. It was close to ten miles just to get back to the location of the Wilderness Store and much further to their own cottage. Staying the night did make sense, even if it did make her uneasy. She nodded thankfully.

After dinner, Victoria cornered Orpine in the hallway. "Please don't leave me alone with Edith. You know how crazy she can get with this conspiracy stuff."

"Don't worry. It won't rub off," he teased.

"Oh, please. The last time we visited, she spent two hours telling me about all the atrocities she believes are going on. Satanic rituals, child sacrifices, one-world government conspiracies. It was disgusting. I didn't sleep for two nights!"

"Just stay with us," Orpine suggested, a little irritated. She hated that she was bothering him with such a trivial matter, but she also blamed him to some extent for having such crazy friends.

After the table was cleared and dinner cleaned up, Victoria asked the question everyone was wondering. "Ralph, when are you planning to rebuild?"

"Can't." He shook his head, staring into the unlit fireplace, his jaw set.

She looked at him, as did everyone else, including Judy. The Wilderness Store was their only source for supplies.

"My supply lines are all cut off," he said. "No place to get stock."

Victoria glanced around the room. "Orpine is out of Trioxin. Where is he going to get a refill?"

Ralph looked worried and sad. After a long pause, he shook his head and whispered. "I'll be damned if I know."

"He's not the only one," Cappy remarked. "Lots of vets need Trioxin. There's gotta be a way for them to get it."

Edith frowned. "Unless they want them all to die."

Victoria looked at Orpine, hating the alarm that she felt burning inside her. Surely Edith was mistaken. Why would she say such a horrible thing? "Who would want our vets to die?" she asked, instantly regretting her question. It was inviting another lecture from Edith, the last thing she wanted to hear right now.

"They do," Edith said resolutely. "They do."

They? The authorities? Our own government? That's just nuts! Victoria was glad she'd only thought this, and not spoken aloud. She didn't realize how much her expression gave away her thoughts.

Ralph glanced at Orpine who just shrugged. "She's still skeptical," he said.

"Well, she better wise up. The government is not our friend!"

The sting from the day's losses came across in his intonation, and Victoria knew he didn't mean it personally towards her. It was anger and frustration speaking, lashing out, as anyone helpless in such a situation would be inclined to do. Unlike Edith who seemed to make it her personal mission to argue with her, and to prove her point.

"They aren't going to stop until we're all dead, vets and everyone else!" Edith declared. "We are their worst enemy because we have the Truth. They want to destroy all of us. It's part of their scheme to control the whole world. It's too late now. It's already happening, just as it was prophesied, and there's no going back."

"That's crazy," Victoria said. "We can go back anytime we want to. We haven't done anything wrong."

"No one goes back," Edith said.

"Daria did," Ralph corrected.

Edith grimaced. "Well, she paid for it, didn't she?"

"What do you mean?" Victoria asked. "Daria left and

went back? When?"

"She went back about 6 months ago," Judy said. "Quite an ordeal, so we heard, what with going through the trial and all. She almost lost her two children in the process and they said she was an unfit mother because she brought them out here away from civilization."

"Trial? Why was there a trial?" Victoria asked, confused.

"Non-conformity." Ralph stated gruffly. "Didn't follow the rules is what for."

"And now they have her. She belongs to them," Edith said.

"But, she did go back," Ralph restated. "Shows you still can if you really have a mind to."

"She only did it for her kids," Edith said. "Some people will do anything for their kids. If you ask me, she's sacrificing them and she doesn't even realize it. They are doomed in Satan's society."

Victoria swallowed. Her muscles tensed and her chest tightened with emotion. "How can you sit there and judge Daria? You have no children of your own. How can you judge anyone?"

Edith replied instantly. "I count my barren womb a blessing from God. It is better to be without children in the End Days when the Great Tribulation comes upon the earth, and we have to flee into the wilderness for safety."

"We are already in the wilderness," Victoria said.

"When they attack, we are going to flee in all directions, just as it is prophesied. What we're doing now is nothing compared to what is coming. Then we will be truly living in the wild. This is just preparation and training." Edith spoke with total confidence.

Orpine glanced at Victoria and sensed he needed to change the subject. "Hey, Ralph, if you're not going to be in the mercantile business anymore, what are you going to do with all your free time?"

"I can think of a few things. Might even get up your way. Hear the fishing is real good," Ralph said, picking up on Orpine's cue.

Victoria sat silently listening to their conversation. *They're all paranoid. I wish I could get Orpine to go away from this place and these people. Daria was the only person I could talk to and now she's gone. I don't blame her. I know she went along with her husband's decision to live out here in the wilderness just like me, but she wasn't a religious fanatic like Edith. She used to complain about all the conspiracy stuff, too. It's too bad he died in that accident. It must have been awful for her and the children. So tragic. I'm amazed she didn't leave sooner.*

She watched Orpine talking to Ralph and Cappy. Edith and Judy were engrossed in some bizarre discussion about the latest conspiracy. *I never should have agreed to come here. I should have known you can't run away from your problems. You only replace them with more problems. If only Orpine would leave-I'd go in a minute. He believes this conspiracy stuff too. He thinks they're really coming after us.*

That night Victoria tossed and turned in a fitful sleep, waking to muffled sounds coming from the bedroom next door. She slipped out of bed and went over closer to the wall to listen and find out what was wrong. Judy was sobbing.

"It'll be all right," she heard Ralph say.

"But Coralee is gone, Ralph, and we've lost everything!"

"Coralee is okay, Judy. She said in her note she was visiting her friends. We'll go and get her back as soon as we figure out where to bring her back to."

Victoria realized that Coralee must have run away. It was an awful scene that night when Judy and Ralph confronted their daughter about the drugs. She almost wished she hadn't told them, but she knew she had to in order to help Coralee. It's difficult enough to be a teenager without this extreme situation. She couldn't help but wonder why Ralph and Judy didn't seem to understand their daughter's needs better, and thought perhaps they did, but couldn't find a solution. It might be easier to deny to

69

themselves the reality that Coralee needed other companionship than just her parents.

"I'll make it up to you, I promise," Ralph said to Judy.

"I'm scared. It's not that they destroyed the Wilderness Store and everything we've worked so hard to build. I'm afraid they will come after us next and that they will take Coralee away from us."

Victoria thought Judy and Ralph might already have lost Coralee, and just didn't realize it yet.

"I'll protect you," Ralph insisted. "I'd never let anything happen to you and Coralee."

"But Ralph, it's all gone. Everything we ever had. Our whole life's work was in that store. It's gone."

"I'll make it up to you," he said again. "I promise."

Victoria thought Ralph was sobbing. She suddenly felt guilty eves dropping on her friend's private conversation but couldn't pull herself away. *Others were having doubts, too.* She now knew that she wasn't the only one.

"We can never rebuild, Ralph. It will take too long."

"I've got the rest of my life if I live that long," Ralph said.

Judy was crying.

"Try not to worry. We'll figure out something."

"I want to go back," Judy said suddenly. "I want to take Coralee and return."

Victoria couldn't believe Judy said such a thing. Judy? The True Believer.

"We're not going back. We're not giving up. I'm not letting those bastards win!" Ralph said.

"But if we wait, it may be too late," Judy pleaded.

"It's already too late."

Victoria went back to her bed and stared at the ceiling for a long while before falling back to sleep. A strange sense of foreboding filled her. No one ever questioned living here before—none of Orpine's friends ever wavered, at least not in front of others. Of course, she'd overheard Ralph and Judy's private conversation.

Could the authorities really be cracking down on the militia and wilderness survivalists? Why? One thing she knew was that Edith wouldn't share Judy's doubts. Never.

The next morning, Victoria woke to voices outside the cabin. She went to the window to investigate and saw a column of militia personnel marching in the early morning sunlight.

Ralph had gone outside and she watched as he greeted the commander who signaled his troops to relax. She got an idea and quickly threw on her clothes and hurried outside.

As she passed female soldiers, she smiled, noticing they were so young, probably still teenagers. She thought it must be exciting for them, out here in the crisp morning air believing they were doing something important. It must give them a sense of purpose and a mission in life, she concluded.

She ran over to Ralph's side and he introduced her to the commanders.

"How many Veterans in your group?" she asked, to Ralph's surprise.

"Quite a few," the commander answered, eyeing her suspiciously.

"How many of them have R.I.T.S.?"

"Quite a few," he repeated, frowning at Ralph.

"She'll all right," Ralph said, understanding now what Victoria was getting at. "I think she's hoping some of your Vets can spare a little of their Trioxin for her husband. He's all out."

The commander bristled. "I can't give my soldiers an order like that."

"Oh, no. Not an order," Victoria said quickly. "If any of them could spare just a little so my husband can survive until he can refill his own prescription. With the destruction of Ralph's Wilderness Store yesterday, our supply has been cut off."

The commander shrugged. "Well, you can ask." "Attention! Everyone." The soldiers stopped talking and listened. "This woman has a request. She's going to ask you a question. Please give her your attention."

Victoria stepped forward. "How many of you have R.I.T.S.?" she asked, noticing Orpine watching from the bedroom window. A dozen people raised their hands.

"Can any of you spare some of your Trioxin for my husband? He's all out."

No one answered. They stared straight ahead.

The commander looked at Victoria. "I told you that was asking a lot of these people."

"Just one pill?" She walked down the ranks and looked from one to another as they lowered their heads or looked forward stone-faced. No one offered.

"I don't believe it. You can't share just one pill with a fellow Veteran?"

Orpine came outside and took her arm. "Don't do this, Victoria. I'm not going to take someone else's Trioxin."

Ralph had watched silently. He looked at the commander.

"We have a mission," the commander said, "We must keep ourselves in top health. It's our duty to defend ourselves and our loved ones. There's a lot depending on us. I'm sorry."

"I understand," Ralph said. He followed Orpine and Victoria back inside the cabin and the militia silently moved on.

She held back her tears knowing Orpine was unhappy with her attempt. She wondered bitterly if he still believed these people took care of their own.

Chapter 5

It's Never Easy to Say Good-Bye

Saturday, June 25th

"Thank you for letting us stay for the night," Victoria said to Edith. The slim, wiry woman was cooking pancakes at the kitchen stove. A quart size canning jar full of maple syrup was in the center of the kitchen table.

Without turning around, Edith said, "Sorry, We're all out of coffee. Got tea, though. The water's hot. Help yourself."

Victoria went to her backpack and pulled out a container. She came back into the kitchen and handed the box to Edith. "Here. It's not Colombian Bean, but it tastes pretty good." She hoped to smooth over any hurt feeling from the previous night.

Edith opened the box. "What is it?"

"Baked dandelion root. I use the whole plant. The flowers make a nice wine, the leaves are a great green vegetable when they're young, and the root makes a nice coffee substitute. I dry it for several days, baking it in a low oven with a sprinkle of my special seasoning. Then I grind it up in a pestle." She smiled at Edith. "It takes a lot of time, but I've got lots of that out here."

Edith smiled gratefully. "Smells great," she said. "Cappy will sure thank you."

After breakfast, Orpine and Victoria took their bags back to the jeep and prepared to leave. Quick good-byes and hugs for everyone, and then Victoria opened the front door of the vehicle. There was a small jar on the seat. "What's this?" she said.

Orpine looked at it, knowing instantly that it was Trioxin.

Victoria picked it up. Scribbled on the side of the label was, "Sorry we could only spare a few-hope it helps." There were three pills inside the bottle.

She looked at Orpine, tears welling up in her eyes. "They did give you some. Someone must have come back and left this here while we were eating breakfast."

Orpine looked sad. Victoria wished he was happy, but knew he was thinking that someone had sacrificed their own Trioxin. She realized the militia might have as much difficulty getting the medicine as they.

She opened the bottle and removed a small blue pill. "Here." She handed it to him. He put it in his mouth, and she pulled out a thermos to give him some water. He never said a word, just swallowed and got inside the jeep. Delight jumped in back.

They drove along for some time in silence. Orpine glanced at her several times, finally asking, "What are you thinking about?"

"Huh?"

"You're a hundred miles away," he said.

Victoria smiled at him glad he wasn't angry anymore. "Why did they burn down the Wilderness Store?"

"It wasn't legal," he said.

"How was it not legal? Didn't Ralph keep records and pay taxes?"

Orpine rolled his eyes and gave her a pitiful look.

"If he didn't, he was stupid!" she said.

"He couldn't."

"Couldn't? Why not? I don't understand. Why couldn't he?"

Orpine shook his head, looking straight ahead as he drove. Delight pushed her nose into the front seat, nudging Victoria who absent-mindedly patted her while she studied Orpine's expression.

"Orpine, why couldn't Ralph run a legitimate establishment?"

"Because things have changed Victoria. You'd know that if you'd kept up with the radio and listened instead of always denying everything. Ralph wasn't operating within the new system. He couldn't."

"Most of those short-wave programs are nonsense, Orpine. You said so yourself. Now you believe everything you hear on the radio? Besides, you haven't turned it on in at least two weeks. Is it broken?"

"Got to be careful," he said. "Heard they can use the radio to locate people. Don't want them to know where we are."

"Get real! Why would they want to find anyone out here? What possible threat are we to the government? Unless one of those militia troops goes off the deep end and starts a fight or something. I'd be more afraid of that with some of their extreme conspiracy ideas."

Victoria knew she was only pushing her husband further away, but she couldn't stop her words, hoping he might listen and change his views.

"One of these days you've got to face reality," he said.

"Me? I've got to face reality? You and your friends are the ones who won't face reality!"

"This is reality, Victoria, whether you like it or not. You can't keep running away from it. You can't hide from the truth."

"You're the one who's running away. It was your idea to live in the middle of nowhere." She regretted the words as they left her lips.

He drove silently for a moment. She bit her lip to keep from crying. Finally, breaking the horrible silence, she said softly, "We need supplies. You need Trioxin. That is the reality."

"We'll manage. We have each other."

She sighed. "Reality?" she said. "You call this reality? Running around the woods like primitive people. Waiting for some government attack?"

"Face it, Victoria. Ralph & Judy's store was destroyed by the authorities. Did you see any trial? Was there any regard for his constitutional rights? They don't exist anymore, not for any of us."

Victoria felt frightened. "We'll find another source for supplies," she said, "someone who does comply with the new system. We're not the only ones living way out here."

"I don't think so," Orpine said.

"What will we do?"

"We'll be okay. We'll just have to make do."

"But you need medication. Where are we going to get your Trioxin?"

"I'll be okay."

She wanted to scream, "Who's not facing reality now?" She knew he wouldn't be okay. He had to know it, too. R.I.T.S. (Recurring Infectious Toxemia Syndrome) could only be controlled with Trioxin. It was not curable, despite Shaman Gay Feathers' concoction.

Orpine's slight fever indicated it was already acting up. She bit her lip, trying not to cry. Without the Trioxin, Orpine would die. That was something she was certain about, and she knew he knew it, too. That was why he was so insistent on her learning to be self-sufficient, so she could survive without him. It wouldn't take long for the disease to kill. *Damn that war!   Why did Orpine have to come back with that disease? Why did the government make it impossible for him to get Trioxin? Why?*

They arrived home late that night after replacing the jeep and hiking back to the cabin. She'd insisted he take a second pill midafternoon when he pulled over to let her drive. He had to be feeling pretty badly to do that.

Even with the second dose, he didn't improve. The long hike took its toll on both of them. Orpine was winded and slow. She helped him the last mile as he leaned on her. Both collapsed, exhausted, into bed as soon as they got inside. Delight slept close by on the floor next to the bed.

The next morning, Sunday the 26th of June, Victoria made coffee while she waited for Orpine to wake up. She had fallen asleep when they got home, but woke in the middle of the night, listening to Orpine's labored breathing. She worried and fretted unable to go back to sleep.

Delight sat obediently on the floor next to Victoria's chair. She obeyed when Victoria told her to be quiet.

Victoria knew what she must do.

Orpine opened his eyes and smiled at her. "How long have you been up?"

She poured him some coffee. "A while."

He sat up and she handed him the cup. "How are you feeling?"

"Been better," he said weakly. "Don't worry. I'll be okay. Just need some rest." He sipped the coffee.

She noticed he was still breathing heavily, as if his lungs were congested. His brow was wet from perspiration. She felt his forehead. "You're burning up."

He leaned forward as she re-arranged the pillows to support him and then rested back.

She sat down in the chair next to him and looked him in the eye. "I'm going back."

"What?" he looked alarmed. "You can't do that."

"I'm going back to get your Trioxin."

"You can't. You don't know what's waiting for you." He shook his head emphatically.

"You'll die without Trioxin. I have to go back. You know that."

He looked at her sadly. He did know she was right. "It doesn't matter about me, Victoria. I'm not afraid to die. I'm afraid to leave you alone." He choked and paused for a moment.

Victoria pressed her lips together tightly, suppressing tears.

Orpine took a breath. "Everything in nature dies at its appointed time. Only men resist this truth. I'm not afraid to die, Victoria. You've made my life so full, much fuller than I ever imagined it could be. I'm only afraid for you. I want you to live, even if,"

She put her finger over his lip. "Shhh. I'll be all right." She smiled through the tears flowing down her face. "You know, I never believed all that hub-bub about the authorities. No one's after us, Orpine. We haven't broken any laws. No one's after me. Why would they be? We have a legal lease from the paper company to be here."

He whispered, eyes closed, "Because you're a non-conformer."

She took the cup and put it aside on the stand. "You rest. We can talk about this later. She bent down and kissed his forehead, noticing how hot he felt. Another large tear rolled down her cheek. "Promise me you won't leave me," she whispered.

"Promise me you won't leave me, Victoria. Promise?" he said, reaching for her hand, holding it affectionately. "Have I told you lately that I love you?"

She swallowed. "I'll always be with you. I love you."

Victoria worried, watching Orpine. He'd slept all day. She didn't want to disturb him and hoped the rest would restore his strength so he could go with her back to medical care and Trioxin.

Surely the Veteran's Hospital would fix him up if they could just get there.

But he slept all day and through the night, Victoria and Delight sitting next to the bed, she on the chair, and the dog next to her, whining periodically, sensing something was terribly wrong.

The next morning he was even weaker. The last pill was used with no noticeable improvement. She made some soup and spoon-fed him, but he ate little. She filled a pitcher of water and placed it on the table next to him. His breathing was heavy and congested. His fever grew worse. She knew time was running out. She couldn't wait any longer and there was no way he could go with her.

She cast one last look around the cabin where they'd lived for nearly seven years. She wondered what changes she'd encounter in her brief visit back to civilization to get his Trioxin. She put an X on the calendar hanging on the wall next to the bed. It was Monday, June 27th. She'd be back by Wednesday, the 29th at the latest. Two days was enough time to accomplish her mission—to get his Trioxin.

She bent over her sleeping husband and kissed his forehead. "Hang on. I'll be back as quickly as I can. Please hang on." She put the pen back on the desk and took one more look at Orpine.

Victoria picked up the small bag she'd packed just before dawn. She didn't need much, just a change of clothes and some of the money from their cache. Three thousand dollars should be more than enough, she felt certain, but then she reached inside the money box and took five gold coins remembering Orpine had said only gold and silver would be valuable currency soon. In case he was right, she decided to put some in her pocket. She picked up the jeep keys and the empty prescription jar.

"Delight, you have to stay with Orpine." She patted the dog affectionately, giving her a big hug. The dog whined and wagged her tail. Victoria had left several dishes of dog food and ample water on the floor near the bed. She put a board in front of the doggie door, knowing Delight would eventually dig it off, giving her time to leave.

She stood over Orpine who slept turned away from her. She bent down and kissed him lightly one last time, mouthing a good-bye, I love you. The dog jumped up on the bed next to him and put her head on Orpine's back. "Take care of him for me," she whispered.

A tear fell down Orpine's cheek when Victoria left. "I love you, too," he said. "Be careful." He stared at the wall. She was gone and didn't hear him.

Victoria grabbed a large backpack on the porch and her smaller bag from inside and headed towards their vehicle, wiping the tears from her face. She took one last look back at the cabin before entering the woods.

"Please, God. Don't let him die out here all alone."

She hurried, wondering if she would ever see her husband again, alive.

Chapter 6

Returning to Civilization

Victoria turned the ignition after replacing the distributor cap, glad she'd watched Orpine do it so many times before. The jeep coughed and sputtered and finally started. She noted the gas tank gage was one quarter full. In the back she had another tank with about 4 gallons that Cappy had provided. *I hope it's enough.* She drove down the old tote road, this time heading towards civilization.

Six hours later, ignoring her growing fatigue, she turned onto a regular paved road, the first she'd seen in nearly seven years. She'd forgotten how smooth it was to ride along a real road. The gas tank gage was empty. She stopped to put the rest of the gas into the tank remembering Orpine telling her that you can't let it run out completely or it won't start easily.

She' slept little over the previous few nights and her body wanted rest, but concern for Orpine kept her going forward. Unlike the gas tank, she couldn't just refuel, though she wished she could.

Victoria got back inside the jeep and pulled out an old paper road map. She traced her route and smiled. I should easily make it by nightfall, and I'll get gas there, at that small town. She focused for a moment on the position on the map where she was pointing as if to let it sink in, then looked around and headed back out onto the highway.

An hour later she passed a young woman with a backpack. She stopped the jeep and backed up. It was Coralee.

Coralee recognized her, but kept walking, picking up her pace.

"Stop," Victoria called, running after her. When she caught up to the girl, she took her arm.

"Stop, Coralee. Where are you going?"

"I'm going away," she said. "As far away as I can get."

"Your parents think you're with your friends. They will be worried about you."

"Let them worry," the girl said with a sniff, and started walking.

"Wait, why don't you come with me? It's not safe to be out here all alone."

Coralee eyed the jeep. It was obvious she'd been walking for a long time. "Where are you heading?" she asked.

"Just into town to get Orpine's Trioxin."

"And you promise you won't try to force me to go back?"

"No."

"How can I trust you? You told on me already."

"I will only tell your folks that you're okay, so they won't worry. You don't want them to worry, do you?"

"Okay, I'll ride with you, just until the first town."

Victoria smiled. "Great. Get in. Let's go."

Two hours later, they passed rural homes. The fuel tank was low. Victoria bit her nails hoping she'd make it to the gas station hoping there would be a gas station somewhere out here. She brightened when she spotted one up ahead in a small village square. It was the little town she'd pinpointed on the map earlier. She pulled into the lot feeling encouraged.

"I'm going to the restroom," Coralee said, jumping out of the jeep when it stopped.

Victoria looked around and pulled over to a self-serve pump, got out and opened her gas tank. When she squeezed the nozzle, the pump didn't work. Exasperated, she went over to read the instructions. It looked simple enough. She was just tired and mechanical things always acted up when one was tired, she reasoned.

SELECT GAS

ENTER S.I.N.

LIFT NOZZLE

BEGIN PUMPING

SELECT GAS/she did. ENTER S.I.N/she shrugged. *What is that?* LIFT nozzle/she did. BEGIN PUMPING/but nothing happened when she squeezed the nozzle. She frowned.

There was no place for her credit card, only a small round black scanner.

"What is a S.I.N.?" she muttered. She tried swishing her card across the scanner again, but it didn't work. It just beeped as if annoyed at her. *We've been gone so long; my card is probably cancelled. Maybe it needs to be activated.*

She noticed another customer at the pump next to her. He was an older man and was watching her. She smiled nervously at him. *My inspection sticker is old. It's expired for sure and my jeep isn't legal to drive. How could I have not thought of that? What difference does it make-I couldn't change it anyway? I think he noticed. Jeez, I hope he doesn't say anything!*

Victoria reread the gas instructions again, avoiding eye contact with the customer. Finally, she shrugged and replaced the pump.

"That's just great. They're always changing these things!" she grumbled as she went inside to get help. *This is an unnecessary delay. Where is Coralee? I wonder if she's hungry.*

Several other customers were inside the store. Victoria took note of them as she entered, suddenly acutely away that she was a stranger. It surprised her how foreign it felt to be back after so long. She wondered if they were also curious about her.

A woman in the far aisle had a youngster in tow as she studied the baked goods. Two young men, probably in their early twenties, were at the cooler, she guessed, getting beer. It was warm outside.

An old man stood in the back. She couldn't decide if he was a customer or an employee, but he seemed to be looking at her, making her a little more self-conscious.

A woman pushed through the door behind her.

"Excuse me," she said curtly, giving Victoria a would- you-please-move look.

"Oh, I'm sorry," Victoria said, standing aside to let her pass.

The woman wore dark reflective sunglasses and Victoria couldn't tell if she was looking at her or not. She was dressed in a fitted outfit that looked like leather, but Victoria was sure it wasn't since animal clothing of any sort had been outlawed before they left for the wilderness. She figured it must be artificial, and admired how smart the woman looked. She realized her own clothing was dingy and worn. Feeling conspicuous, she tidied her hair nervously and looked away from the woman.

Victoria took a breath, resolved to get a few supplies with her gas. She gathered some fruit and juice in a small carriage. Then she smiled. Barbecue potato chips-her favorite. She hadn't eaten any in years and suddenly craved them. She would indulge. She put the bag in her carriage, then reached for a second bag and added it before heading for the checkout counter.

The old man turned out to be a customer and now stood in line ahead of her. The two young men fell in behind her and the woman and child behind them. It seemed everyone was ready to check out at the same moment.

Victoria waited uneasily in line, anxious to be on her way, wondering where Coralee had gone. She watched the old man put his items on the counter.

Huh?   Interesting innovation. Must be a scanner. She watched as the man's items were scanned into the machine and then the man held his hand over the round black scanner just like the one on the gas pump. She watched, intrigued. The clerk thanked him and the man picked up his goods and headed out.

No money. Imagine. How did he pay for that? I didn't see any money. He must have used a credit card. Maybe I just missed that part. She shrugged and stepped forward to empty her carriage onto the counter. She placed two fifty-dollar bills down in front of the clerk. "I need some gas, too, but I can't figure out how to use your pump."

The room was suddenly dead silent. The clerk glared at her.

She waited, shifting her weight, wondering why he wasn't taking her money. There was a video camera focused on her from behind the counter. She felt even more self-conscious.

"Is this some kind of joke?" he boomed. His complexion grew pink and Victoria wondered if he were more embarrassed, or just angry. Both, she decided, but she didn't know why.

"What is the problem?" she asked, examining her money.

"What are you trying to pull?"

"I'm not pulling anything!"

He studied her intently. She felt the stares of the others in line behind her. She glanced around and saw the woman with the child huddled in the back of the row, holding her little girl close as if trying to hide the child's eyes from some awful sight. The two young men were keenly watching her.

She gulped. The woman in the leather outfit stood in the back near a rack of tabloids as if oblivious to what was happening.

"You're serious, aren't you?" the clerk asked.

She nodded, puzzled.

"Lady, I don't know what your angle is. What are you, some kind of government agent? You're not going to entrap me! I've heard about this! No sir, I'm not going to fall for it!"

"I don't understand. What's wrong? I just need some gas."

He reached for the phone. Victoria felt alarm surging through her body. She picked up her two fifties. "If you don't want my money, I'll just find another store where they're not so rude."

"Grab her!" the clerk ordered. "I'm calling the BCT."

The two young men lunged for Victoria, each taking an arm and holding her tightly. She couldn't escape.

"What are you doing? Let me go!"

The clerk watched her closely and entered a phone number. He smirked. "I'm gonna collect a big reward for this!"

"Hey, not so quick," one of the young men said. "We want part of the reward, too. We're holding her for you."

"Reward? What are you talking about? You must have me confused with someone else," Victoria said, struggling to free herself.

The woman with the child looked disgusted. "Ugh! She's one of them. A Cling-On! Don't even look at her," she said to her child, pulling her and exiting the store quickly.

"Don't panic, folks," the woman in leather said with authority. She still had on her sunglasses. She stepped forward holding out an intricate badge, bronze against navy blue suede. "I'm B.C.T. and I'll take over now."

Everyone was silent, watching the woman fearfully. "No way. We want the reward," the clerk said. The two men nodded nervously.

"You people think you're in control? I know how to handle these rejects," the woman bellowed with surprising authority. "I got control of this situation. Is that clear? I'm in control! Are any of you challenging me?"

The two young men immediately released their hold on Victoria. The B.C.T. agent grabbed her arm, pinching her.

"Ouch," Victoria cried.

"Give the clerk you S.I.N.," the agent told the two young men, holding her badge up to the video camera for a few seconds. She reached over the scanner with her hand. "I'll see that you're all included in the reward."

The two men stood back and watched as the official escorted Victoria outside.

Victoria looked around desperately as the agent pulled her towards a vehicle parked behind her jeep. She didn't resist the agent.

"Can you please tell me what is going on? Did I do something wrong? This is all a misunderstanding. I've been away for a long time, for several years."

The woman ignored her. When they got to the car, she opened the door and ordered Victoria, "Stay right here." She released her grip on Victoria's arm. The agent reached inside to her radio and to grab some restraints.

Victoria watched with alarm as the woman brought the restraints out of her compartment. She looked at her jeep. The gas pump was still in the tank. She pushed the agent into her car and slammed the door, sprinted to her jeep and jumped inside. There was no sign of Coralee and she couldn't wait now. She turned the ignition and sped out of the parking lot, down the road as fast as she could, tearing the nozzle from the tank and dragging it like a tail behind her.

She looked in her mirror and saw the two young men and clerk running outside, yelling at the B.C.T. official and pointing in her direction.

She turned the corner out of sight. Sure to be pursued, she turned down a rough side road, slipped her jeep into four-wheel drive and drove as far as she could over fields and through the woods until her jeep stalled from lack of fuel.

She pounded her fists on the steering wheel. Then she gathered her bag and money from the back seat, jumped out of the jeep, and sprinted deeper into the woods.

Victoria didn't stop running for nearly an hour. Finally she rested at the top of a small, wooded hill. Walking slowly, she caught her breath. No one seemed to be following and gradually she calmed down.

She thought of Orpine back in the cabin and wondered how he was doing. Delight would have gotten outside by now. Orpine would be low on water and she was glad she'd left some extra bottles near his bed.

Suddenly she feared he wouldn't find them, or worse, wouldn't be able to lift them. She stopped and took a deep breath. *I have to be positive. I have to believe he's still alive!*

When she got down the other side of the hill, Victoria stopped at a stream to take a sip of water. Her long braid fell forward. She studied her reflection in the water and wondered if the B.C.T. agent was still looking for her, remembering the video cameras back at the store.

She reached into her pocket and took out the gray plastic knife Orpine had given her. It was slipping through the tear in the bottom of her pocket, only half of it still inside. She stood up and breathed deeply, then cut off her long braid. Her hair fell instantly in loose curls around her shoulders.

The knife was surprisingly sharp so she trimmed the front, adding bangs. Using the water for a mirror, she dampened her hair and finger combed it in place. She examined her new look. *Not bad.* It was uneven but she smiled, satisfied she had changed her appearance, just in case anyone came looking for her.

I'm getting as paranoid as Orpine and his friends. She frowned. *What if they are right?*

She splashed water on her face and washed her hands, then scavenged for some roots and berries to eat.

She leaned against a large red oak tree and, fatigued from lack of sleep combined with the warmth of the late afternoon sun, she dozed.

Victoria felt something tickling her arm and then her abdomen as she awoke from a deep sleep. Instinctively, she brushed it away.

She heard giggles, which startled her back to reality, and she jumped, pushing her back against the tree, scraping on the rough bark.

A little boy and a little girl stood in front of her, holding the stick they'd used to poke at her.

"Who are you?" she asked.

"Who are you?" a tall, thin man asked, coming from behind the children. "Robin and Jeremy, you come back over here." They ignored him and continued to stare at her. She sat up and brushed the dirt off her pants.

"My name's Victoria."

"It's her. It's the lady from the store, Jeremey said, standing closer to the man and pointing at her. She won- dared if he was their father, but somehow didn't think so.

"I shouldn't have run away. I got scared. I'm going to go back and explain to them it's all a misunderstanding."

He laughed. "Sure. They'll believe you."

"If I turn myself in,"

"And make it easy for them. Don't you know the law?"

She pondered for a moment, studying the man. "Who are you?"

He didn't answer.

Victoria stood up and the two children clung closer to the man. "I'm not going to hurt you. Gosh, I'm just here to get Trioxin for my husband."

"Trioxin? Your husband must be a Vet?"

"Yes. He is."

"Where are you from?"

"North," Victoria said warily. "Where are you from?"

Again, he ignored her question. She felt uneasy being the only one providing information. She brushed off her clothes. "I have to get out of here. Orpine won't last much longer. I have to get back with his medication." She started to walk away.

"Where are you going?" the man called after her.

"Back to the store."

"They won't listen."

She stopped and turned around. "Why?"

Who is this man? He was dressed like a city pedestrian, not a hiker or naturalist. He didn't fit out here, and the children were well dressed and unsoiled. They looked like they'd just come from school and he from work.

He shook his head. "You'll be arrested the minute they spot you. Bet you got money on you, too. Don't you?"

Victoria clutched her bag, giving herself away.

"Ha! You don't have a prayer!"

"I have to get Trioxin for my husband. He's completely out and he's getting very sick."

"Come with us. Maybe someone will help you."

"Where are you going?"

He started down the trail without answering, the two children following close behind. She frowned, irritated that he didn't answer, then sighed, with a quick glance back towards town, reluctantly went after them.

She lagged behind but kept them in sight. Carefully she reached into her bag and retrieved one of the gold coins and hid it in her bra. After glancing ahead to make sure they hadn't seen her, she repeated with another coin, until she had hidden all five of them.

Robin came skipping back towards her and took her hand. Victoria was pleased with the youngster's sudden friendliness. "So, you're Robin?"

She nodded.

"That's a pretty name."

"My Mommy named me that cause she said the first thing she saw after I was born was a robin. It's her favorite bird."

"What a nice story." Victoria held the little girl's hand a little snugger, smiling.

"I lost my dolly."

"You did? Where did you lose it?

The little girl shrugged. "I don't know. Somewhere when we moved."

"What's taking so long?" Jeremy called as they waited for the two to catch up.

Robin let go of her hand and ran ahead. Victoria quickened her pace soon catching up. Without a word, they continued on.

An hour later they approached an encampment in the middle of the woods. Huts and tents that looked to have been recently erected rather quickly filled the area below the tree cover. Victoria hesitated, surveying the area, and lagged behind the man and two children.

"Come on. I'll introduce you," the man called.

Robin and Jeremy ran ahead, greeted by other children who recognized them.

She shook her head. "I don't know."

"It's okay. Come with me."

"I don't think so. I don't know these people. I don't even know your name."

"My name is Danny. There's nothing to be afraid of here. Come on."

Reluctantly, she followed him. She'd seen this type of encampment before, people all dressed the same, all thinking the same things. She wondered which was worst: her fundamentalist friends or these communal dropouts.

Children pointed at her and adults stopped whatever they were doing to stare at Victoria as she followed Danny through the camp towards a large hut in the center.

A man dressed in army fatigues stepped outside the hut as they approached.

"Are you crazy, Danny? Why did you bring her here?"

Danny glanced sheepishly at Victoria. "I think she's okay. She doesn't seem to know anything about the system."

The man in authority glared at Victoria. "Wait here!"

He turned around and Danny followed him inside the tent. "Don't ever take it on yourself to bring a stranger here. You've endangered all of us. Now we'll have to move again. You know we've been here barely two weeks. What were you thinking? I thought you had more sense than that! How can I ever give you leadership roles when you make dumb decisions like this?" The man yelled so loudly he might as well have stayed outside the tent.

"I'm real sorry, Master," Danny said.

Victoria shifted nervously as people stared or scowled at her. *I knew this was a mistake. I gotta get out of here!*

"Bring her inside!"

Danny came out of the tent. "Master wants to talk to you."

"Maybe I should just leave," Victoria said as she picked up her bag.

"No. You must talk to Master first." She could see a plea in his eyes and for his sake, agreed. She followed him back inside the tent.

The Master sat behind a large desk that seemed out of place in a tent setting. She wondered how they moved it.

"Who are you?" he demanded.

"Victoria."

"Where are you from, Victoria?" he snarled.

"North of here. Look, I don't mean you any harm," she started to say.

"QUIET. Just answer my questions."

She grit her teeth. "Sure. What do you want to know?"

"Exactly what are you doing here?"

"I'm here to get Trioxin for my husband. He has R.I.T.S. and he's dying. I am in a big hurry." She could barely believe she'd said Orpine was dying. Speaking the words aloud had sharpened the reality.

Master eyed her suspiciously. "Take her bag, Danny." Danny stepped towards her.

"No." She clutched her bag.

"I told you it'd get you into trouble," Danny whispered as he took her bag and handed it to Master.

She glared at Danny. "I never should have trusted you!"

Master pulled out a fist of money, then dumped the entire contents on his large desk. She saw rage growing on Master's face. Something else, too, was it some sort of sinister delight? Victoria glared at Danny who squirmed nervously.

"Looks like we're going to have a big celebration tonight," Master said, spitting the words at Victoria. "You must be one of them. A Cling-On! How despicable. Maybe we can help you overcome your sinful ways."

"I'm not the least bit interested in overcoming what you think is sinful about my ways." She could contain herself no longer. "I know all about your kind. I respect your right to believe whatever you want. I really do, but I don't share those beliefs or ideas, and I don't have to. You're not my Master! I need my money and I need to get out of here. NOW!"

"You should show respect for Master," Danny whispered helpfully.

"He's not my master!"

Master stood up and smiled confidently, as if in complete control. "We don't try to convert anyone. People see the light when they are ready. You, obviously, aren't ready, yet."

"So I can go?"

"Not yet."

"I'm in a hurry."

"You can leave when we're ready to move on. It won't be more than three weeks. We just got here."

"I can't stay here for three weeks. I told you, my husband is dying. Don't you understand that I have to get him Trioxin? There's no time to waste."

"We have our own worries. You're an outsider. Your problems are of no concern to us." He shook his finger towards her to dismiss her.

She reached for her bag, but he grabbed her arm.

"Get her out of here, Danny!"

"It's my money. You can't just steal it from me."

Danny tugged her away. "Come on. It won't do you any good anyway."

Danny led Victoria to another tent near the outskirts of the village. Inside dream catchers hung on the side walls and candles glowed in the corners.

"This is Marelle." Victoria heard children playing outside in the back. "She's Robin and Jeremy's mother," he said, smiling at the woman.

Marelle was dressed in earth-toned pants and tunic with turquoise beads draped around her neck. Victoria surmised the two were close friends, and that she had been correct, Danny was not the children's father.

"Master wants you to make our guest comfortable," he said.

"Come inside," the woman said. "I'll make some rose hip tea."

"I'm no guest," Victoria muttered.

Danny and Marelle looked embarrassed.

"I'm sorry about Master," Danny said. "I thought sure he'd help since you were in trouble with the authorities."

"Why didn't he?" Marelle asked.

"She has currency."

"Oh," Marelle said with a startled look.

Danny left the tent. Marelle boiled water for tea over a small gas-powered camping stove.

Victoria paced back and forth. "I can't stay here. Time is running out!"

"Well, you have to wait until Master gives permission to leave."

"You don't understand. My husband is sick and he's going to die. I can't just wait around for three weeks for your Master to decide it's okay for me to leave. Who does he think he is, anyway?"

Marelle was silent. Victoria knew she was upsetting her. She sat down. "So, Robin and Jeremy are your children?"

"Yes," Marelle said.

"Is Danny their father?"

Marelle blushed. "No. Their father is an unbeliever. He left four years ago when Robin was born. He's never been back. We're divorced now."

"I'm sorry."

"Don't be. It's part of my reality. That's what Master says. We're hoping he gives permission soon so Danny and I can be joined. Then he will be Robin and Jeremy's father. Master has the strongest spirit guide of anyone I've ever known."

"Spirit guide?"

"Uh, huh. My husband left because he couldn't communicate with his own inner spirit guide. That's what Master told me. Not to worry. Everyone comes around in their own due course. Danny has been a wonderful friend. We know we're intended, as soon as Master gives permission."

"You don't need Master's permission. You don't need anyone's permission. Why don't you two just get married? It's your life."

"You obviously don't understand," Marelle said softly. Victoria knew what she meant, just as Edith had meant, if you don't share her beliefs you must be an unbeliever. Victoria understood more than Marelle realized. She'd met many communers among Orpine's friends. They lived in wilderness camps like this one. Even Orpine thought they were irrational in their worshipping the earth and listening to spirit guides.

"Why did Master take my money?" Victoria knew there was no convincing this young woman of her folly, but she desperately needed to get out of here as soon as she could. "If Master is so pure and good, why would he steal my money?"

"He didn't steal your money. He confiscated it. That's the law. He had no other choice. It's illegal to possess currency. You must know that you aren't supposed to have any money. That's the law." She looked at Victoria, puzzled.

"The law? Danny said that, too. What law?"

"Where have you been? The law that makes currency illegal. Everyone uses their S.I.N. now. Currency has been outlawed for five years."

"S.I.N.?" Victoria remembered the gas pump. Marelle held out her hand. "Right here, on my hand. It's implanted. My individual and unique State Identification Number. S.I.N."

"Sounds like a cattle brand to me," Victoria said, studying the woman's hand. "I don't see anything."

"You can't see it. It's under the skin. Just like here, on my forehead."

"Why on your forehead?"

"In case this one gets damaged. It's a double-check. I don't know exactly how they work, but the two go together so no one can duplicate yours. Don't you have a S.I.N.?"

"No."

"Where have you been?" Marelle repeated.

"I've been up north in the Allagash wilderness with my husband, Orpine, for the last seven years."

"Wow. That's cool. All by yourself? No children?"

Victoria swallowed. "No. Just Delight, our Golden Retriever, and Yerba, our cat."

"Cool."

"If I can't use money anymore, how am I going to get the Trioxin? Where can I get one of those S.I.N.'s?"

"I don't know. They were issued years ago. Everyone has them by now, except a few dissidents. Money lovers. Cling-ons!"

Victoria was surprised by Marelle's sudden scorn. "Who?"

"There's a whole underground society. People who still use currency for trade. They cling to the old ways, but the B.C.T. is cleaning them up. It's a big issue because they are hurting the rest of society. Money lovers!"

"I don't get it, Marelle. Money lovers? B.C.T.? What are you talking about?"

Don't you know? The love of money is the root of all evil. The B.C.T. is the Bureau of Consumer Trade. They enforce all the currency laws."

"It's not money that's evil, Marelle. It's the love of money. There is a big difference. Greed is what's evil and you can have greed without money. Greed for other things like power and control. Like Master."

"Master has integrity!" Marelle said.

Victoria knew she'd struck a nerve.

"If there's no money, what is there? How do you buy things?"

"It's all done on the Consumer Trade Network-the C.T.N. Everyone has an account and the network keeps track of additions and subtractions."

"And no more privacy," Victoria said.

"What do you mean?"

"You just told me that everything is recorded on the Consumer Trade Network. That means someone can know everything you buy-everything about you. You have no more secrets and no more privacy."

"Only if the system is abused. There are laws to protect against that. Besides, why should we hide what we're doing?"

"Maybe you don't want others to know your business?" Victoria said.

"It's a much better system now. There's no more cheating on taxes, no more stealing, everyone is honest."

"Then why the B.C.T.?"

"Human nature. Someone always finds a way to beat the system. Like the money lovers and the Cling-Ons."

"I wonder what happens when the power goes out?"

Marelle looked puzzled.

"You know, if everything is done on a computer network, what happens if the power goes out or there is some sort of glitch?"

"They have all kinds or protections. I don't think we should discuss this. No one beats the system. We shouldn't even be talking about that."

Victoria figured that was all the information she'd get from Marelle. The children came inside and their conversation ended.

Robin climbed onto Victoria's lap. "Can you tell me a story?"

Victoria smiled.

"Maybe Victoria's tired and doesn't want to tell stories right now," Marelle said.

"That's okay. I'd love to tell Robin a story. What kind of story do you like?"

The little girl shrugged. "A happy story."

"Well, let's see. Do you know the one about the cat and the fiddle?"

Robin shook her head.

"It goes like this: Hey diddle, diddle, the cat and the fiddle,"

Robin laughed. "What's a fiddle?"

"It's a musical instrument. You put it under your chin like this and pull a wand over the strings to make a sound." She tickled the little girls chin and Robin giggled.

"What else? Tell me the rest of the story?"

"Hey diddle, diddle, the cat and the fiddle; the cow jumped over the moon."

"How does a cow jump over the moon? Is this a true story?"

Victoria laughed at Robin's childish innocence. "Let me finish. The cow jumped over the moon. The little dog laughed to see such sport, and the dish ran away with the spoon!"

"Do dishes run away?" Robin asked.

"Well, I guess they do in fairy tales."

"That's only a make-believe story?"

"That's right," Victoria said. "Do you want to say the poem with me?"

"I don't know how."

"Just follow me. I'll teach you."

Victoria repeated the poem and soon Robin had it memorized. She jumped off her lap and ran over to Jeremy to tell it to him.

"She's adorable," Victoria told Marelle.

"You're good with children. Too bad you don't have any of your own."

Victoria looked away silently. Marelle sensed her pain but wasn't going to pry.

"I had a little girl," Victoria said softly. "Her name was Colleen."

Marelle waited respectfully knowing she was about to tell her something very personal.

"You remember the Crystal Swamp incident?"

"Yes. I was a teenager then, but I remember it on the news. Everyone was talking about it at the time."

"We lived there. My husband was away most of the time, stationed overseas. So it was just Colleen and me. At first I didn't believe the neighbors. They were convinced pollution was killing all the pets. Dogs and cats disappeared. Some thought it was a giant alligator or something."

Marelle stopped preparing food and sat down opposite Victoria. "What happened?"

"It turned out the dogs and cats were being taken by the authorities for testing. They knew all along it was dangerous for anyone to be living there, but they never admitted it, right up until the end, until it was too late." She paused.

"I stayed, even after most of our neighbors had left. I thought they were just over-reacting. Sure, I found flowers and vegetables that were deformed. They looked odd, with strange shapes and colors. I thought it was just some freak of nature, not something that would affect humans. The government scientists insisted there was no pollution. They assured us there was no danger. The truth is we didn't have anywhere else to go. Our home was all we owned and with the rumors, you couldn't give the property away. In the end, I left. I got an apartment, but it was too late. I should have left when the others did."

She wiped away a tear. "My first husband came home when Colleen got sick. Our marriage ended after she passed away. He never said so, but I know he blamed me."

"What happened to your daughter?"

"She went quickly. She was the first, you know. In the end, eleven children died and several more were left severely disabled. For some reason, the younger they were, the quicker it progressed. Cancer. The doctors couldn't do anything for her. It was all my fault. If only I'd left sooner."

"You can't know that would have made any difference. Did any of the other children that got sick leave before you?"

"Yes. They all did. But still, I can't help but wonder if it would have turned out differently if only I'd listened sooner and got out."

Marelle reached for Victoria's hand. "You shouldn't blame yourself. You didn't cause the pollution."

Victoria wondered why she was telling this complete stranger so much about herself, but it felt good to discuss it. "I wanted to die. It was the worse experience you can imagine. I thought I could never be happy again. I thought the pain would never go away."

"Maybe you can't let the pain go away?"

"You could be right. Maybe it's all I have left of Colleen."

"Did the government ever admit their mistake?"

Victoria nodded. "They paid us for our property. I kept my half and invested it. A year later I met Orpine. He made me smile again. He sings to me." She smiled at Marelle.

"That's how we got here. We used the money to lease the land we live on from the Paper Company. That and Orpine's military disability. He's sick now and I have to save him. I can't lose him. I can't fail him."

"You're brave," Marelle said. "I could never endure losing one of my children."

"I didn't have much choice. Nothing brave about it. It's life. And it stinks!"

"You shouldn't think like that. Guilt is most destructive. Besides, this is all part of your reality."

"My reality? Are you suggesting that somehow I chose for my child to die?"

The young woman nodded. "Your higher self decided you needed to experience these things long before you even became a human."

"I needed to experience the death of my child? For my own personal development? Is that what you believe? Don't you see that as a bit selfish?"

"But it serves no purpose to assign blame. That's what Master says. Blame is destructive. Everything happens because we chose it. We may not understand why now, but our higher self knows."

Victoria sighed deeply. "You really believe this stuff, don't you?"

Marelle nodded. "So you see, life only seems bad to you at this time. It really isn't. Someday you will understand everything. Isn't that wonderful?"

"Only seems bad? Are you saying it really isn't bad? I'd like to know what you think bad is?"

"There is no good or bad," Marelle stated.

"Come on. That's so simplistic."

"Reality is what you create in your own mind. There isn't really any good or evil. There's no right or wrong. Some things are positive, and some are negative. That's all. Guilt and blame are negative. Master teaches us great wisdom."

"Master speaks a lot of horse shit!"

"You don't understand. You're not in touch with your natural spirit. It takes time to commune with nature. That's understandable with all you've experienced."

"Aww, come on. Do you really want Robin and Jeremy to grow up believing there is no right or wrong?"

"I just want them to be free spirits."

"Freedom doesn't mean lack of responsibility."

Marelle shrugged.

Victoria had felt rage at Edith's simplicity, but somehow with Marelle, she was more patient, perhaps because Marelle seemed so young and innocent, so trusting. Even so, it was obvious that no amount of reasoning would convince her to change anything in her beliefs. Maybe she was wrong to even try. Was she any happier?

Danny popped his head inside the tent. "Hey, you better hurry. The celebration is about to start. Master is trancing BIG TIME!"

Victoria could only watch helplessly as Master held up her money in both hands, ranting to the crowd circled around him. He sat in an old wooden spindle chair that was out of place in the woods. It belongs at a kitchen table. He rolled his head and spoke in broken words she couldn't understand.

"What's he on?" she said to those next to her, but no one paid her any attention.

The group chanted, too, swaying and holding up their hands. Suddenly, Master jumped out of his chair.

"He's got the spirit!" a man next to Victoria cried. Everyone cheered.

"Listen, he's saying something," a woman said.

The crowd grew quiet.

"Evil!" Master cried. "Evil! There is evil among us."

"Evil, Evil," the crowd chanted.

"Money is the evil in society," he yelled, spitting out the words. His hair flew about his wild eyes. "We must root out all the evil," he cried.

"Evil, Evil," the crowd chanted.

"Take this," he said, throwing the money at the crowd. "Help me root out this evil from among us!"

They grabbed at the money in a frenzy. He began to dance around. The people followed behind him, chanting, "evil, evil, root out the evil!"

He lit some bills and held them up. The crowd hushed. The paper burned completely in his hand. "Burn away the evil in your hearts," he said in a quiet voice.

The man next to Victoria whispered, "it's the spirit. He's got the spirit good tonight."

Master lit another bill and held it up until it burned completely. The people were mesmerized. "Root out the evil!" he yelled, lighting another and tossing it into the fire pit in the center.

Everyone mimicked him, lighting the money they'd grabbed and tossing it into the pit. The frenzy continued as they whooped and leapt around the fire.

"I thought you said there was no good or evil," Victoria said to Marelle.

Marelle looked down sadly. Victoria walked back to the hut.

"I have to leave first thing in the morning," Victoria told Marelle when she returned to the tent.

Marelle told Robin and Jeremy to go to bed. "You can't leave tomorrow," she said to Victoria.

"Yes I can. I have to. Is Master going to lock me up like a prisoner? I'm leaving!"

Marelle looked Victoria squarely in the eye. "Master will restrain you if you try to leave tomorrow."

Victoria was stunned. "First he steals my money. Granted it isn't worth anything, but it still belonged to me. Then he burns it up in some fitful ritual. Now he's going to hold me against my will? He's going to hold me hostage?"

"You must leave tonight," Marelle whispered.

Victoria looked at her in shock. Marelle nodded affirmatively. "You can't wait until tomorrow. Master will sleep tonight. He's always exhausted after a trance. But tomorrow, he will hold you here."

"Okay, then. I'll leave tonight. I'll leave now."

"Here," Marelle said, handing her several fifties she'd saved from the celebration. "I don't know what help this will be to you. Maybe you can get your husband's medication."

Victoria paused for a long moment, realizing what Marelle had done, the leap she'd made in her own reality. Maybe there was hope for her new young friend.

"Thank you."

"Go east, through the path in the opposite direction you came in. I will take you to the path as soon as the children are asleep. Go about eight miles and you will come to another town. Hopefully, no one will know who you are there. You'd be wise to stay away from the one you were at when Danny found you. They're all in a tizzy. Everyone wants to get the reward."

Marelle looked down sadly. She whispered, "I think Master wants the reward, too."

Victoria took Marelle's hand. "I wish there was something I could do for you. You are going to get in trouble for this, aren't you?"

"I'll just say you sneaked out in the night. Who's to know? Besides, getting in trouble is not in my reality." They giggled.

Victoria followed Marelle to the path. She paused for a moment, both of them standing silently in the moonlight. The village was quiet now, except for a few barking dogs in the distance.

"Good luck with Danny," she said, "I hope everything works out for you. Thank you for helping me."

"Thanks. My children are the most important thing in my life. I just want them to be happy."

"They are lucky to have you for their mother. Marelle, did you ever think that maybe this commune is a bit fanatical?"

"One person's fanaticism is another person's faith," Marelle said. "Faith gets us by when reality gets tough."

Victoria nodded. "We all do what we have to do. I guess I understand."

Marelle reached into her pouch and handed Victoria a smooth flat stone. "Here, take this. It's always brought me good luck."

"What is it?" Victoria held the flashlight on it and could make out pinkish shades and facial features.

"It's an amulet, symbolic of mother earth. When we learn to love our mother, we are free to love ourselves and each other."

"Thank you. Don't you want to keep this?"

"I've got lots of amulets. I want you to have this one. It will connect us wherever we go. I know it was destined that our paths should cross."

Victoria put the stone in her pocket with the gray plastic knife. It immediately fell through the hole in her jacket pocket, lodging inside the lining.

"You better hurry before someone sees us," Marelle said, glancing around. Victoria gave her a quick hug and turned down the path.

"Good luck. I hope you find the Trioxin."

Chapter 7

Wednesday, June 29th

It was after midnight when Victoria headed down the path where Marelle had directed her. She thought about the young mother and her two children and it occurred to her that she'd been able to interact with Robin without the dire results she'd feared.

She felt good that a little bit of her burden lifted just knowing that she was able to share moments with children again. It'd been so long. She was thankful to Marelle for that as well, even though she knew Marelle was unaware of her ordeal.

She didn't need the flashlight because it was a cloudless, full moon light night. It was slow going as she carefully avoided rocks and fallen limbs. She pressed the light on her watch. It glowed bright green. She squinted and saw that it was 1:27 AM, Wednesday, June 29th.

"It's been over 24 hours since I left Orpine. I hope he's all right."

Her voice sounded strange in the backdrop of a nighttime forest. *No time to be afraid.* She walked on, fretting. "Maybe I should have stayed with him. If I fail to get the Trioxin, he'll die anyway, all alone." The idea was unbearable and she wiped away a tear.

"I've got to think positively," she said to herself. "I've got to devise a plan. Orpine taught me that. This is survival. What would he do? What would he want me to do?"

Talking aloud helped her focus and made the hike a little less lonely and scary. She suddenly missed Delight.

"What are my choices? I could get my own S.I.N., maybe, if I can figure out how without getting arrested again. Perhaps I can find a sympathetic doctor who will provide me with the Trioxin. The Veterans' Administration Hospital might help. Surely, they must have Orpine's' medical records."

She walked further in silence. She stopped and looked up at the moon. "If I have to, I'll steal the Trioxin." She walked along.

"Some plan, Victoria. One thing for sure, I'm running out of time!"

Victoria approached a clearing in the woods up ahead just as the first rays of morning sunshine peeked over the horizon in a light pink hue. She squinted first left, then right. The rural road she'd come to seemed to lead nowhere.

She slumped to the ground, overcome with fatigue. "What am I supposed to do?" she cried. "Oh, God, what am I supposed to do? When I follow the rules, my daughter dies. Now I don't conform and Opine is dying. What am I supposed to do? Please, dear God, don't let Opine die!"

Exhausted, Victoria curled up on a dry patch of pine needles beside the road. She rubbed her aching ankles. "I just need to rest for a little while," she said to herself.

She set her watch alarm for one hour and was immediately sound asleep. When it beeped an hour later, she stood up and stretched, surprised as how stiff she felt. She looked both ways and decided to head south. Before long she came to a large sign:

WELCOME TO PHALAROPE LANDING

A sketch of a duck was inscribed underneath the words. "I sure hope this is a friendly town," she muttered as she passed the sign.

A mile down the road, an old truck slowed down behind her. It was the first sign of life she'd seen. She walked on nervously, hoping the truck would pass by if she ignored it.

"Hey there, young lady. You're a long way out here by yourself. Need a ride?"

Victoria glanced at the old man and decided he looked harmless. She smiled. "How far is it to town?"

"Bout six more miles. Hop in. I'll give you a ride as far as my farm."

"How far is that?"

"Four miles, more or less. You wanna walk the whole ways, go on ahead. Ride's offered if'n you want it."

She hesitated.

"Ain't got all day, Miss."

She opened the door and climbed in. The seat was hard with the vinyl torn in the seams from years of use. He drove on, shifting a squeaky gearshift as they bounced over the bumps.

"Thanks for the ride," she said.

"Don't mention it."

"Sure beats walking." She couldn't think of anything to say. She glanced at the man in her peripheral vision, not wanting to stare. He wore farmer clothes, heavy work boots that were tied with a strip of leather around the ankle. It looked like rawhide, but of course, she knew it couldn't be.

His red plaid woolen jacket was weathered and had a warm comfortable look to it. His beard was short and all gray, matching his thick curly gray hair. It was almost white, reminding her of Santa Claus. *Must be his off-season job-helping wayward soul*, she thought.

Seeing his passenger smile was his cue. "How far you been walking? I didn't see no broken-down vehicle back there anywhere."

"I came a different way," she said.

"That so?"

A few minutes later they turned into the driveway of an old, run-down farm. It looked barely habitable, yet an elderly woman was hanging towels on the clothesline.

"Won't you come on inside and meet the missus?"

"I really have to be going," Victoria said.

"Suit yourself, but she'd got some nice hot blueberry muffins in the oven 'bout ready to come out. Good 'n hot. Nice creamery butter, too. Hard to walk far on an empty stomach. You'll make much better time if'n you eat something first."

He eyed Victoria from the corner of his eyes. "Sure you wouldn't like to meet the missus? She loves to feed folks, especially strays."

Victoria smiled. "Well, I am hungry now that you mention it. You sure it won't be any bother?"

"Wouldn't have offered if t'were." The old man's eyes twinkled.

She got out of his truck and closed the door.

"Who'd you bring home with you?" his wife called from over the clothesline, scrutinizing their guest.

He looked at Victoria. "Well, a lady in distress, and kind'a hungry, too, by the looks of her. She's been walking this morning and won't say how far. Facts the case, I'd guess quite some distance."

The old lady came over to them and reached out to Victoria. "Hi, dear. My name is Val." She smiled warmly and then glanced questioningly at her husband. "What did you say her name was, Warren?"

"Don't knows that she told me."

"Victoria. My name is Victoria. It's nice to meet you Val. Your husband was kind to give me a ride. I really appreciate it. I'm in a hurry."

"Not too much of a hurry as to miss out on one of your hot blueberry muffins, though," the old man said, winking at his wife.

"Well then, you timed that just right. They're about to come out of the oven just now. Come on inside, dear. Rest a bit. You look like you could use some nourishment. Warrens' right, the muffins are almost ready."

"I told you my missus likes to feed strays," Warren said to Victoria with a grin.

Victoria entered their old worn kitchen. It had a warmth that seemed to emanate from it creating a loved and well-kept look. She imagined there had been many years of warm, fresh-baked muffins served in this kitchen.

"You sit right down," Val said. "I'll get the coffee."

The bright morning sunlight filled the cozy room and Victoria realized it was still very early in the day, only a little past six. The aroma of the brewing coffee and baking muffins accentuated her hunger pangs and she was even more grateful for their kindness.

"I haven't had real coffee in a long time," Victoria said.

"What other kind of coffee is there?" Warren asked.

"I make my own from dandelion root. It's actually quite good once you get used to it."

"You ain't one of those gypsies, are you?" he grunted.

"Warren!" Val scolded. "Of course she isn't. Besides, they don't like to be called gypsies. Now mind your manners."

"I'm not a communer," Victoria said, laughing. "No, that's for sure. Not a naturalist, either, if that's what they still call themselves."

"Well, I'm glad to hear that," Warren said.

"To each his own. Anyway, that's what I always say," Val said, glancing at her husband.

He shrugged. "Just wondering, that's all. No crime in curiosity is they? Seems like everything's a crime these days."

Val gave him a stern look.

"Besides, they wouldn't be living so fancy free and all if the government weren't handing out those credits every month. Just encourages free loading, that's what it does," he said.

"Credits?"

Val glanced at Warren and Victoria realized she was supposed to understand what he was talking about. She felt her face blush.

"Credits? You know, that new-fangled Electronic Currency."

"E-Cash," Val interjected, "for those of us who remember when we carried our money in our pockets." She patted her apron pocket as a gesture to accent her comment.

"Every month your account gets credited with the minimum allotment. Supposed to equalize things somehow. Danged if I can figure out how it does, though. Facts the case, I can't figure it out for the life of me. It sounds more like taking from the workers and giving to the bums!"

"Been a lot of changes over the years," Val said.

"Ayah, facts the case, we sure have seen a lot of changes," Warren said. "Bet you don't even remember what it was like when good old American Currency was all we used, back in the days when people paid cash when they wanted something."

"In God we trust," Val said, nodding.

Victoria smiled. "Do those credit things have to be paid back?"

Warren laughed. "Credit? Guess it could be mistaken for a loan, couldn't it? No. The way they explained it to me, it's just there to spend. Supposed to replace welfare and unemployment benefits. Anyone who doesn't get a minimum wage income gets credits every month. How else could folks live like gypsies?"

Val looked at him again.

"Nomads? How could they live like nomads?" He gave her an is-that-better look.

"If it is credit, then wouldn't the government be incurring more debt. Where does the money come from? What backs it up?" Victoria asked.

"Got a good point there, young lady. Facts the case, nothing in life is ever free when you get right down to it. Folks don't think of the credits as debt, but someday all that credit is going to have to be paid for by someone. Now that's something to think long and hard about ."

"It's all part of the Consumer Trade Network, you know, the new system," Val said.

"And we thought we beat communism way back when I was a young man!"

Val gave Warren a stern look.

"Where are you heading, dear?" she asked Victoria.

"Town."

"Phalarope Landing? Not much there."

"I have to get Trioxin."

"You a Vet?" Warren asked.

"No. It's for my husband, Orpine. He's sick."

"R.I.T.S. That's bad stuff," Val said.

"I have to get his prescription refilled and get it back to him."

"Back where?" Val asked.

Victoria hesitated.

"Now you're the one asking too many questions," Warren said. "Fact's the case, she don't need to tell us none of her business at all if she don't want to. We ain't nosy folks."

"That's okay," Victoria said.

"Your husband, Orpine, must have been in the Euro/ Asia War. That was a bad one," Warren said, shaking his head sadly. "Very bad. Worse than Afghanistan."

"Are you a Vet?" Victoria asked.

"He was in Iraq, back in the late 1990's."

"That was a long time ago. I remember learning about that war when I was in high school," Victoria said, calculating the old man must be in his 80's. *He looked pretty good*, she thought. *Probably Val takes good care of him.*

"They don't teach you the truth in school," Warren grunted.

"Warren," Val scolded.

"Umph!"

"I know what you mean," Victoria said, thinking about Ralph and Orpine and their other veteran friends. "Orpine doesn't like what happened either. He says the government knew what they were doing to us over there and still sent in the troops. He says it was all politics."

Warren frowned. "Got that right, young lady. Facts the case, a GI's life ain't worth a damn! Not when compared to some politician's career. That's for sure. That's the facts all right."

"I guess that is the fact," Victoria said.

"That's right. Glad to see a young lady like yourself understand those facts."

"Young, huh?" Victoria smiled. "Sometimes I don't think I'm so young."

"Val here is getting close to seventy-eight," Warren said, giving his wife a playful pinch.

"Well, I guess thirty-seven seems young compared to seventy-eight. I just hope I look as good as you when I reach your age."

"Thirty-seven? Don't say. I'd never guess. You don't look no more than twenty-five," Val said.

"Must be all that fresh air," Warren said. "Look at her nice tan."

"Must be," Val agreed.

"Not a city girl, that's for sure," Warren observed. "You sure you ain't one of those gypsies?"

"Warren! Really, that's enough. Here are your muffins. Dig in while they're hot."

"Could be worse," Warren said.

"What could be worse?" Victoria asked.

"Could be one of those militia-survivalist types. A Cling-On."

Victoria blushed. "No. I don't fit there, either."

"You might as well ride into town with me, young lady," Warren said as they went back outside after breakfast. He decided he needed some things at the hardware store.

"Good luck, dear," Val called from the kitchen sink.

"Thanks for the muffins and coffee," Victoria called back to her.

Victoria climbed inside the truck and waved good-bye to Val. "Those were the best muffins I ever ate," she said to Warren.

He smiled and waved to his wife who waved back from the kitchen window. "Well, you come back and visit us again, and bring that husband of yours with you," he said.

Warren parked his truck in front of a small pharmacy. "This must be your destination," he said, turning the engine off.

She climbed out of the truck and turned toward the old man. "Thank you again for the ride and everything." She suddenly wished she didn't have to be alone.

Warren smiled as if he understood. "You take care now. Stop in and see me and the missus next time you're in town. You're always welcome."

He started his truck and headed towards the hardware store. She watched him drive away.

Here in the center of this small town she felt totally lost. The wilderness was familiar to her now; this was foreign. She wondered how to approach the pharmacist. What if they asked for her S.I.N.? She gathered her resolve and pushed the door open and headed inside the pharmacy.

Victoria looked around and was thankful there were no other customers in the store as she approached the counter.

"May I help you?" a young woman asked.

"I need to get a refill of my husband's prescription." She handed the clerk the empty container and said. "It's for Trioxin."

The clerk studied the jar and looked at Victoria. "This prescription is several years old."

"I know. We've been away. Do you carry Trioxin?"

"Well, we have it for several veterans in town. It's special ordered from the city. You know it's a highly regulated drug and we don't carry any extra."

"But it's an emergency. My husband ran out and now he's too sick to come back to the hospital. All I need is enough for him to recover sufficiently to return for treatment at the Veteran's Hospital."

The clerk looked sympathetic. "I'm really sorry, but I can't give you someone else's prescription, not even part of it. That's against the law and they're real strict about enforcement. They even do spot checks and count the number of tablets in our inventory."

"What if you ask one of the other Vets if they'd be willing to lend us some?"

"I can't do that."

"Why not?"

"It's just not allowed. Trioxin is regulated. It 's against the law to give it away under any circumstances."

Victoria knew the young woman wasn't able to help her even if she really wanted to. "Well, what are my options? I've got to get Trioxin. I'm desperate. My husband will die soon if I don't find it for him."

"You could have the prescription renewed and get your own supply in the city."

"How?"

"All I have to do is enter your S.I.N. into the computer and send it to the Veteran's Center."

"My S.I.N.?"

"Well, it should be your husbands, but since he's sick, maybe they'll accept yours, especially if I fax them a copy of this prescription. All they would have to do is verify it from the prescribing physician." She looked at the date doubtfully.

"Can't you just fax the prescription without using my S.I.N.?"

"How will you pay for it?"

"I don't suppose you take credit cards?"

The clerk laughed nervously.

Victoria said, "Let me see if I can get a ride to the city, to this Veterans' Center. If not, I'll come back. Thanks for your help."

The clerk handed the empty bottle back to Victoria. "Good luck. I hope you get it in time. I'm sorry I couldn't be more helpful."

"I wonder where this city is," Victoria said to herself as she walked down the sidewalk wishing she'd taken her road map when she abandoned the jeep. Warren's truck was still parked in front of the hardware store. She headed towards him.

He came out carrying a bag. He saw her. "Well, did you get what you needed?"

"Not exactly. How far is it to the city? To the Veteran's Center?"

He frowned and turned to put his bag in the truck, then turned back around to face her. "Facts the case, there ain't no roads from here to there," he kidded.

"Really, Warren, how far?" She sounded desperate.

"Too far to walk, that's for sure. It's about 40 miles to Woodinville. But the roads ain't very good. Will take you an hour, maybe a little more, by vehicle that is, on a good day. Little longer if you're planning to hike all the way."

"I can't get Orpine's Trioxin with a new prescription. The lady at the pharmacy said I needed to get it from the Veteran's Center in the city. They only have enough to fill prescriptions for the Vets in town and can't give me any of it, not even enough to help Orpine recover and come back for treatment."

Warren looked at her thoughtfully. "Let's go back and see if I can have some better success. I know Tilly pretty well."

They both entered the pharmacy. "How you doing today, Tilly?"

"Fine, Warren. How are you and Val doing out on the farm?"

"We're doing just fine as usual. My friend here has a problem."

Tilly looked at Victoria. "I tried to help her, Warren, but there's no way I can give her anyone else's Trioxin. It's against the law. I will lose my license and my business. You know I'd like to help, but I can't.

"Well, there must be some way. She'd kind of desperate you know. Her husband's real sick. Time is of the essence."

Tilly thought for a moment. "I told her I could order from the Veteran's Center with her own S.I.N., but she didn't want to do that."

Warren glanced at Victoria and surmised the situation. "Well, now, here, use my S.I.N. Would you give that a try for us, Tilly?"

"I'm not sure," she said, hesitating.

"Scan it in there. What harm can that do?"

She scanned the bar code on Orpine's medicine bottle and entered Warren's S.I.N as he passed his hand over the scanner. "I don't know about this, Warren. I don't think this is a good idea."

"Nonsense."

He winked at Victoria and she smiled back.

After a moment, a cold, impersonal message scrolled across Tilly's computer screen. They all read it.

UNAUTHORIZED CODE NUMBER. REQUEST DENIED.

"I told you it wouldn't work."

"No harm in trying, Tilly. Facts the case, there's got to be a solution to this young women's dilemma."

Tilly eyed her suspiciously. "Why doesn't she use her own S.I.N.?"

Victoria blushed.

Warren took Victoria's arm. "Thanks for all you help Tilly. I'll tell Val you said Hi." They exited the pharmacy quickly.

"Thank you for trying to help. I don't know what to do. I have to get to the city."

"Did Tilly tell you the names of any of those Vets that uses Trioxin here in town?"

"No."

He clicked his jaw shut and waved to her to get into the truck. She did. He drove to a diner near the outskirts of town and parked out front. "Come with me. Let's see if we can find one of those Vets for you."

She followed Warren into the seedy diner. He surveyed the room, his countenance glum, then brightened at the sight of a man in the far corner booth. As he headed towards him, he held out his hand.

"Mel! How's things going? Mind if we join ya?"

Mel eyed Victoria while he shook Warren's hand. She thought he was much older than Orpine, if he was a vet of the Euro/Asia War. Warren and Victoria sat down across from Mel, her on the inside of the booth.

"Who's your friend?"

"This here is Victoria. Her husband is a vet of the Euro War, like you." Warren waited for the information to register with Mel.

Mel took a bite of his ham and eggs and chewed it. He swallowed. "So?"

"He's sick. Real sick. Needs Trioxin." Warren nodded at Victoria.

"He has R.I.T.S. and ran out of Trioxin. I'm here to get him some more."

Mel studied her as he took another bite.

"You know any vets around here that use Trioxin and might loan her a small amount just to help him out?"

"Nope."

Warren squinted his eyes and banged his fist on the table, rattling Mel's dishes. "Come on, Mel. For once in your life, do something for someone else. What's the matter with you? Ain't I helped you out of enough jams that you can do this one little favor for me?"

"No can do, Warren. Only have enough to last until my next prescription. That's the way they do it. That's how they keep tabs on what us Vets are up to."

"You can't spare just a few tablets?" Warren asked in a quieter tone.

"Trioxin is regulated. You know that. They don't give us no extra. I'll die without my dosage and it ain't a pretty death, either. I seen it. No way am I parting with my Trioxin, not with one tablet! No way."

A tear fell down Victoria's cheek but she ignored it. She glared at Mel. "Orpine would have done it for you. He wouldn't have thought twice about it, even if he didn't know you."

"Oh yeah? And why is that?" Mel glared back.

"Because you're a Vet of the Euro/Asia War, just like him."

Mel swallowed and she thought she detected a hint of shame on his face. It quickly faded. "Well, I ain't as good as your Orpine."

Warren and Victoria watched as Mel chewed another bite of food. It was obvious he wasn't enjoying it as he sloshed it around his mouth like dry sawdust. "Why can't he get his own Trioxin anyway? What is he, some kind of criminal or something?"

Victoria blinked. "Of course not! We live up north in the Allagash woods. We haven't been back in several years and up till now he was able to get it from a store there. But the store burned down and now he's all out and we can't get it." She knew she was rambling but couldn't stop. "We're not criminals!"

Warren looked at Mel with disgust. "Come on, Victoria," he said, taking her arm. "He ain't going to help anyone but himself. Facts the case, he's a used-up, has-been, and precious little good to start out with." They slid out of the booth.

Mel sat silently, looking straight ahead. "You could get some from the Central Distribution Warehouse at Woodinville. Least, that's what I've heard."

"What?" Victoria asked, turning around.

"Come on. He's crazy. You can't do no such thing. He's been smoking too much dope," Warren said.

"Well, I guess that depends on just how desperate you really are," Mel said. He looked at his coffee and took a sip with a smirk.

Victoria sat back down. "It's okay Warren."

"Sounds like this lady is real desperate," Mel said.

"Victoria, you don't wanna get mixed up with this guy."

"It's okay. I'll be fine."

Mel waved Warren away. "The lady and me have business. Be on your way old man, so we can talk private." Victoria looked at Warren. The wrinkles on his aged face seemed deeper and longer and she knew he was worried.

"I will be all right, Warren. Thank you for all your help."

"I didn't bring you here to get you into no trouble," he said, giving Mel a glare.

She stood back up. "I'll be okay." She gave him a hug and whispered, "thank you for everything. Don't worry. I'll come back and visit you when this is all over."

"You sure," he said doubtfully.

She nodded. "You go. No need for you to be part of this."

"Just watch yourself, young lady. Mel here is a real snake!"

"I will."

After Warren left, Mel looked up at Victoria, picking his teeth with his fork. "Old fart!" he said, "always minding other people's business."

"Warren's a nice old man, and so is his wife."

"Ha!" He stared at her and for a moment she wished Warren had stayed.

"You're one of them, aren't you?"

"I don't know what you're talking about."

"You're a Cling-On. You're one of those holdouts who don't want to change for nobody."

"No. I told you who I am. We live along in the Allagash wilderness."

"Bet you don't got no S.I.N., do you?" She blushed.

He smiled. "But maybe you got money? How much?" She remembered the Master's celebration and sighed.

"Not as much as I started out with. Two hundred dollars." She pulled it out of her pocked and showed it to him.

"Are you crazy, lady? Put that away before someone sees it."

She put it back into her pocket and glanced around. No one had noticed.

He looked at her long and hard. She wondered if he was satisfied with the amount or trying to decide if she were telling him the truth.

"Forget it."

"I can give you more," she said quickly. "More of that worthless paper? Forget it?"

"I have coins back at the cabin," she said.

"I need a down payment," he said.

"How much?"

"How much? That's a good one! A thousand dollars might be a good place to start. Better yet, gold or silver. You got any of that?"

"Gold?"

"Currency won't be good much longer," he snickered. "No one uses it anymore. There won't be any left, except in museums. And that will be worthless. Hell, it's worthless now. You got gold, lady?"

She reached for the silver coins hidden in her bra while he watched. She handed him the five coins.

"Well, this is better. How much more do you have on ya?"

"That's all. I don't have any more with me."

"Well, correct me if I'm wrong, but didn't I see some gold in there with these silver coins?" He pointed at her blouse.

She blushed and pulled out the locket. She didn't want to trust this man, how could she? He was obviously a scoundrel. But time was running out.

Victoria took the locket off her neck. This is gold. I'd let you keep it as security if you help me get the Trioxin.

Mel reached over to examine it, getting much to close for her comfort. She avoided his gaze. "Nice locket. But I need gold coins."

"I've got plenty of coins back at the cabin. I'll give you all you want once Orpine has his medicine."

"How do I know that?"

"Well, take these," she said, handing him the silver coins and her locket. "Just remember, I want the locket back when I pay you the coins at the cabin. They're worth a lot more than this locket."

He examined it closely, curiously.

"It has sentimental value," she said, "and I want it back. It's your guarantee that I'll pay you the rest of the money at the cabin, after we get the Trioxin to my husband."

"I'm listening," Mel said. "You got my interest, but how do I know you have the money?"

"We cashed out everything we owned when we left seven years ago. We've only used a little so there's plenty to pay you if you help me."

She could see the greed in his eyes. "The love of money," she said.

"What?"

"Nothing. Just something someone told me last night. Are you going to help me or not?"

He grinned. "You just bought yourself a deal, Lady."

Victoria had second thoughts as they drove along in Mel's old car. It sputtered and backfired constantly. He was a terrible driver. She wondered if it was lack of skill, brain damage from the war, drugs, or maybe a combination of all three. He'd taken a long time in the men's room before they left, and maybe taken some kind of drug.

When they swerved over to the other side of the road rounding a corner, she decided she'd had enough. "Stop the car," she yelled.

"You wanna drive, lady?"

"Yes. You're the worse driver I've ever had the misfortune to ride with."

"Well, you got it. Here." He stopped the car in the middle of the road and slid over to the center of the seat. She got out and hurried around and got into the driver's side.

"Just go straight," he said, leaning over onto the window and closing his eyes.

She sighed and drove on, praying that they would make it all the way. *Maybe Warren was right*, she thought.

"I would have been better off walking," she said, but Mel didn't hear her. He was sound asleep, or unconscious. She decided it was the latter.

As they approached the city of Woodinville, Victoria noticed a large, newly constructed building, several stories high and very much out of place here in the country. A sign in front read:

REGIONAL PROCESSING CENTER

There were fences all around the building and a guard posted at the entrance at the end of a long driveway. "What have they got in there? Fort Knox?"

"Hey, Mel. Wake up. We're in the city. Which way to the Medical Center?"

He rolled his eyes and bobbed his head, looking about with a glazed expression.

"What are you on, anyway?"

"Go left," he mumbled. "Look for 8th Avenue. It's on 8th Avenue. I think it's on 8th Avenue." He closed his eyes again.

"Jerk," Victoria muttered. Finally she located 8th Avenue. *Which direction?* She could see Mel would be no help. She turned left and went all the way to the end of the street without finding the center. She backtracked all the way to the other end.

There it was. A large metal warehouse with a big sign in front. Orange letters:

VETERAN'S CENTRAL DISTRIBUTION CENTER

Underneath, in small orange letters:

No Unauthorized Admittance

She shook Mel to wake him up after parking along the curb a little further down the street.

"Hey, I'm getting hungry," he said. "Where are we?"

"We're at the distribution center."

"Good Girl. See, I told you we'd find it."

"We?" She shook her head. "What do we do now, Mel?"

"Wait till dark."

"I can see you have this well planned," she said.

"Yeah, right, well planned." He grinned and snorted another dose.

"Will you stop with that stuff! Don't you know it will kill you?" She grabbed it out of his hands and threw it in the back seat, but it was too late. He was already well into his dream state.

He mumbled, "I'm already dead, Lady." He slumped down in the seat and she didn't even try to wake him. Instead, she got out and surveyed the area. She was relieved that he slept. With or without Mel, she was going to get the Trioxin. Preferably without.

When Mel woke, it was getting dark and Victoria was getting ready to go inside the Center.

"You wait here," she instructed as she got out of the car. She reached into her bag and pulled out the prescription bottle. She slipped it into her right jacket pocket along with Marelle's amulet and the gray knife, which was now somewhere in her jacket lining.

"Sure. No problem, lady. I'll wait right here," he drawled.

She looked at him wondering if he could be trusted. She hated to rely on the likes of him for something so important.

"There's lots of gold for you when we get back to my husband," she said.

He looked at her, disgusted, or perhaps insulted. She hoped she hadn't offended him. Then again, maybe he was just ill from his elixir.

"Look, lady, I said I'd wait."

"Victoria," she said.

"Huh?"

"My name isn't lady. It's Victoria."

"Whatever."

Victoria made her way around to the back of the large metal building. A truck was unloading at the dock. She hid in the shadows, watching intently. A guard was talking with the deliveryman and joked about something that happened at an earlier stop. Both men laughed boisterously.

She crouched down and skittered to the front of the big truck, and then stood up slowly and glanced past to see what they were doing.

"Going to be another long night," the guard said, turned towards the doorway, away from the loading dock.

"You on alone again?" the deliveryman asked.

"Yeah. Jim's wife is pretty sick. I cover for him. Poor guy." He shook his head and the other man nodded.

"Must be hard on him, and the kids," he said.

"Is this your last stop tonight?" the guard asked.

"Last one. Easy route this time."

"How about a cup of coffee before you hit the road?"

"Sure. We can fill out the shipping slips inside." They both went inside the building.

Victoria crept closer to the dock. The door was still open and the men disappeared down a long corridor. Silently she made her way up the stairs and slipped inside the door, hiding behind it for a moment to allow her eyes to orient to the bright lights inside the building, and to catch her breath. She was conscious of her breathing and wished she could be quieter, but her adrenaline was pumping.

She looked down the hallway. Everything was bright causing her eyes to smart after being outside in the darkness. Even the unloading area was sterile white and polished.

Victoria's heart pounded as she stepped out from her hiding place. The soles of her shoes squeaked on the waxed floor as she walked and she was afraid the men might hear her. It sounded quite loud because of the echo affect in the empty hallway. She considered taking off her shoes but didn't. It would take too much time and leave her vulnerable in plain sight. Then she'd have to carry them or leave them exposed, so she kept them on and tried to walk as quietly as she could, with little success.

The recent boxes delivered were sitting in a rack further down the hall, still on the pallet. She approached, watching carefully. The two men were together somewhere down this hall. She could hear them chattering in the distance, with intermittent bursts of laughter.

The new shipment had several large boxes. The bar code on the outside of the containers didn't give her any clue as to the contents, so she pried one open. It wasn't Trioxin.

That would have been too easy. Nothing in this whole challenge has been easy. Why should I hope for a break now?

Victoria looked around wondering where the Trioxin might be stored. Then she heard the door open down the hall and the two men walking in her direction. She bolted to the end of the hall and pushed on a door. It was locked. Their footsteps were just around the corner behind her.

She sprinted to another door, even closer to the corner. It was unlocked and she slipped inside just as the men rounded the corner. Her heart pounded as she rested her head against the door, trying not to breathe so hard, and listen intently. The men's voices faded down the corridor. They hadn't seen her.

She sighed in relief and looked around the room, which was dimly lit by an outside streetlight. It was some sort of office with rows of computers. Their little green screen-saver security lights watched her like tiny alien eyes in the dark. She shivered.

Victoria reached towards one of the computers and pressed a button on the keyboard. It beeped and displayed

....AUTHORIZED ACCESS ONLY.... On the screen.

The beep startled her in the quietness of the room and she glanced towards the door to see if the men had heard. It was silent.

She pressed another key and an extensive menu appeared, lighting up the screen. *This is the government computer system. It looks like the mainframe.* She looked quickly to see if she could locate Trioxin, but unfamiliar with the program, soon realized it was a futile effort.

She went back to the door and listened. When she looked back at the computer, the tiny green light was back, blinking at her from the screen. She pressed her ear hard against the door and when the hallway was silent, opened it and peeked out.

No one was in sight, so she exited the computer room. The two men were outside on the loading dock again and could have seen her clearly in the brightly- lit corridor if they had looked in her direction.

She hurried past the opening towards where they had gone for their coffee. She regretted the squeaking of her shoes on the highly polished floor. No time to take them off now and still no place to hide them. She smelled the aroma of the brewing coffee in the cool night air as she passed by the guard's room and its blinking monitors.

There were video cameras in the hallway, which she suddenly noticed. She tried to avoid them when possible and was glad the guard wasn't at this station watching his monitors. Of course, if anyone reviewed the tapes later, she'd be there plain as day. Couldn't worry about that now.

The dock doorway closed with a secure latch that echoed down the quiet halls. She glanced behind and hurried towards the other end of the building. She pushed open a double door and stood inside a huge warehouse with rows of highly stacked boxes, bar-coded on the front placards. No words described their contents, only the barcode. Her heart sank. *How can I find Trioxin in this maze?*

Victoria looked back behind her and couldn't see anyone coming. She scanned the high ceilings. There were more surveillance cameras. She could only hope the guard wouldn't notice her. So far there was no alarm, at least none she could hear.

She pulled out the prescription bottle from her jacket pocket and studied the bar code on the bottom label, trying to make sense out of it. She began to compare it to the placards and realized quickly that none were even close.

She went to the next isle, and the next, with the same results. No Trioxin. It must be here somewhere. Where would they keep dangerous and controlled drugs? Where?

Her watch beeped and she was surprised that she'd been inside for over two hours already. It was nearly 3:30 A.M. And it was Wednesday morning.

Panic overwhelmed her as she thought of Orpine. She'd marked the calendar for him, promising to be back today. And here she was, unable to find the Trioxin.

I've got to focus. I've got to keep calm. She took a deep breath and looked around. At the end of the long warehouse was a small door with an orange sign clearly visible even from this distance.

NO ADMITTANCE.

That must be it! She ran to it and looked around. No one was there. The door was locked and secured by some sort of computer system with a card-key slot on the outside. There was a small window in the door, only about six inches square. She peeked inside. Shelves were stocked with small boxes of drugs. She recognized one of the barcodes and pulled out her bottle. It was Trioxin!

Victoria slid down the door and sat on the floor defeated. There was no way to get into that room. With so little time left, she would have to find another source for the Trioxin.

She wiped a tear from her face, annoyed with her inability to obtain this medicine. She noticed red lights blinking from the hallway and looked up. There were lights blinking on the ceiling, too. Alarms! Silent alarms. Her presence had been detected!

She raced towards the door at the end of the warehouse where she had entered. The guard charged through it. She ran down the aisle trying to hide behind some boxes and listened for his footsteps to determine his location. His shoes squeaked on the shiny floor just like hers did and she knew exactly where he was. When he approached down the aisle opposite her, she crept back down the other side towards the doorway.

"You can't escape!" the guard yelled into the air, testing her mental resolve. "The police are on their way. Probably pulling up right now. There's no way out of here. Make it easy on yourself and give up peacefully."

Victoria tried to time her steps to his words in order to keep him from hearing her shoes. Closer she crept towards the door, listening for the guard. When he headed in the opposite direction down the next aisle, it was her chance to escape. She sprinted towards the door and pushed through it. She ran down the hallway and lunged out the heavy metal back door of the loading dock. It opened surprisingly easy from the inside.

The air had cooled and her breath condensed into miniature clouds as she ran towards Mel. She stopped.

"Where is the car?" She looked around wondering if she'd gone the wrong way. No. There was the curb and street sign where she'd parked earlier.

But no Mel. "Where is he?" She looked left and right. "Damn! I knew I couldn't trust that son-of-a-bitch!" She kicked the curb, hurting her foot a little.

"Hold it right there!"

She turned around and the guard was pointing his gun at her. She raised her hands.

Chapter 8

You never know when it'll come in handy.

Victoria stood there for a moment. "Come this way," the guard ordered, motioning back towards the warehouse with the muzzle of his gun.

"I can explain," she said.

"Quiet. Save your explanations for the B.C.T. They'll be here soon."

She walked back towards the dock looking for an escape route, but he followed close behind keeping a keen watch on her. *He probably wants the reward. He thinks I am some kind of criminal. Probably doesn't get much excitement as a night watchman.*

He took her back to the room where he'd had his coffee earlier. The console was a collection of small videos viewing the areas with which she was now familiar, the hallways and the warehouse. His empty coffee cup sat on the edge of the counter.

"Put your arms on the wall," he barked. She did. He used a scanner to check for weapons and detected none.

"Empty your pockets," he said, pointing towards the counter.

She pulled her right pocket liner out of her jacket and Orpine's prescription jar fell to the floor.

He eyed it nervously, then motioned to her other pocket.

She pulled its lining out, too, but it was empty with threads hanging in the corner where it was torn.

"Sit down." He pointed to a chair with the muzzle of his gun still fixed on her.

She sat down and he secured her hands behind her with a plastic handcuff. He picked up the prescription bottle.

"Trioxin." He looked at her and squinted. "You don't look like a Vet with R.I.T.S. Were you planning to steal some of this?"

"It's for my husband. Check the label. He's very ill."

The guard smirked. "You think I was born yesterday? I know who you are."

"You do?" She was genuinely surprised and wondered if he'd seen her photo from the convenience store. "It's all a mistake. I can explain everything."

"Save it. I know what you're up to. Trioxin is valuable on the underground market. Bunch of losers! Money lovers! Your kind is going to spoil it for us law-abiding citizens. You're despicable!"

"My kind?" She felt rage growing and wanted to free herself to challenge this man. *How dare he judge me? I'm trying to save the life of the man I love. This man and his kind are despicable!*

"You non-conformers. You think you're so smart; you think you know better. Well, it's your kind that causes all the problems for the rest of us. You're nothing but a bunch of greedy, money hungry bums! That's what the whole bunch of you are: a bunch of Cling Ons!"

"I don't suppose you've thought anything about collecting a reward for capturing me and turning me in, now have you?" she chided.

"Reward. Well, good deeds do deserve to be rewarded. Nothing wrong with that."

"You're more greedy than the people you accuse. Why would a reward be offered except to appeal to your own greed?"

"Oh, no," the guard said defensively. "I am a law- abiding citizen. It's your kind that don't follow the law. You steal from the rest of us."

"I haven't stolen from anyone," Victoria said.

"Then what are you doing in this warehouse?"

She frowned. "My husband is dying. Why doesn't anyone listen? I have to bring him Trioxin. He's too sick to travel. Time is running out. It might already be too late."

"You must think I'm stupid?"

"I'm telling you the truth," she cried.

"Non-conformers like you are all a bunch of lying thieves!"

"No. No. You're mistaken. I'm not what you think. I always obey the law. You are mistaken. Please, let me go. Please!"

"You're the one who's made a big mistake. You think your pretty smart, don't you? Well, you're not smart enough, not when they get through with you. You're going to find out just how smart you are and you're going to wish you'd conformed."

"I am an American Citizen. I have rights. They can't do anything to me because I haven't done anything wrong."

The guard turned away, satisfied that he'd tormented his captive, and examined the video equipment.

Victoria felt her jacket inseam with her fingertips. She could barely feel the gray plastic knife next to Marelle's amulet in the lining of her jacket . *Some luck that brought me.* She fingered the knife closer to the tear in her pocket, inching it closer and closer.

The guard turned around and glanced at her. She looked down quietly and sat very still hoping he'd think she'd given up. Some sirens sounded in the road and he looked down the hallway.

"They're here. I'll be right back. Got to unlock the door and let them inside." He smiled smugly at her when he left the room. She heard his steps squeaking as he walked quickly down the antiseptic hallway.

Victoria reached as hard as she could tearing the pocket liner and grabbing the plastic knife. Opening the blade, she was able to cut its way out of her jacket and pull it back behind her.

She cut at the plastic wrist restrains, at first with barely noticeable results. She wasn't sure if it was working at all. She heard the guard unlatch the door down the hallway.

"Right this way," the guard said after greeting several people. Footsteps, like military tap shoes, echoed down the hall.

Victoria worked feverishly. *Come on! Come on!* Finally she cut through the plastic. She jumped up and grabbed the empty Trioxin jar and hurried to an indentation in the wall on the opposite side of the hall.

She hid there in the shadow as the guard led his entourage past her towards his office.

"We've been looking for her for three days," one of the police officers said as they passed by.

"She's been real slick," another added. "Must have been trained well."

"Not a good sign. Boss says they fear the insurrection could start at any minute. They're anxious to interrogate her and find out what's going on."

"It doesn't look good," the other police officer said. "Well, she's been real talkative so far," the guard said. They passed so closely that she held her breath fearing they might hear it. Thoroughly engaged in animated conversation with the guard, they didn't notice her.

Once past, she waited until they approached the office doorway, then dashed down the hall to the dock and slipped out the door trying to latch it quietly.

The guard yelled, "She's got to be here! Secure the area!"

Behind her, she heard the heavy metal door lock with a harsh mechanical click. She'd barely gotten out!

Victoria sprinted down the driveway and across streets as fast as she could trying to stay in the shadows. Police cars passed with their lights flashing furiously. She hid behind some bushes as several more cars approached from another direction. *Jeez. You'd think I was some sort of vicious killer or something.* She timed her escape, running a little further with each opportunity. Soon she was away from the scene.

The sun was rising when Victoria walked down the city streets into the center of Woodinville. She pulled her collar up for warmth, thinking it was a chilly morning for June. She put her hands in her pockets, too.

It had been two hours since her escape from the Distribution Center and she'd walked the dimly lit streets, hiding whenever a vehicle approached, wondering what to do. Surely the police were still searching for her. No way they were going to give up. That was certain.

She passed a bakery and coffee shop just opening up. The aroma of the fresh brewing coffee reminded her how long it had been since she'd eaten. Yesterday, Val's muffins. It seemed so long ago now. Her stomach growled. *Can't even eat.* She glanced down towards her hands and wiggled them inside her pocket. *No S.I.N. My God! What have they done?*

She smiled a little. "They?" she spoke aloud to herself. "Now I'm doing it."

Chapter 9

Thursday, June 30th

Victoria thought about her calendar and Orpine back home in their cabin. She was late. If he was still alive, he must be wondering where she was. *If he is still alive.* She stopped and blinked back her tears. *I can't give up. I can't let him down. I can't.*

When she rounded a corner, she stood opposite the Woodinville Police Station. *How odd? They're all in a tizzy searching for me and here I am, right under their noses! It would be funny if it wasn't so tragic.*

She lingered on the sidewalk, just watching the police station. It didn't make sense to keep running. Where would she go? *Surely they will understand my predicament if I explain it all to them. I never intended to avoid the new currency system. I didn't deliberately break any laws. I didn't even know about the S.I.N. Surely they will understand if I explain it all to them.*

There was little traffic. Slowly, she walked across the street, and paused in front of the police station, looking up the front steps. She took a deep breath and then headed up the steps into the Police Station. *I can do this. It's my only option-I have no choice. It'll work out. Orpine's paranoia has rubbed off on me. I can't get caught up in that anti-government stuff. I haven't done anything wrong--at least not intentionally. I can do this.* She nodded to herself and took a deep breath, opened the door, and went inside.

No one paid any attention to her as she stood in front of the reception desk. She stepped closer. The clock on the wall read 5:45 A.M. She looked around. Two officers were engrossed in animated conversation over in the corner. They didn't notice her. The man behind the desk in front of her was talking on the phone. *What was I so worried about? They don't look threatening. I should have done this in the first place.*

She guessed the shift was just ending and the commotion and activity would wind up soon. She could wait patiently for a few more minutes. Her heartbeat was slowing and her nerves calming. Even her stomach stopped growling.

A small smile broke across her face at the thought her ordeal would soon be over. *These people are no different than we are back in the wilderness. They probably have spouses and children at home. They look like the understanding sort. This isn't so bad.*

Empty Styrofoam coffee cups littered the desk. She hoped the new shift brought a cleaning crew. A voice from behind her brought her back around to the desk she'd turned away from.

"Can I help you, ma'am?"

Victoria looked at the young officer who had spoken to her. Ma'am sounded so old, but she surmised to the young man, it probably seemed appropriate. *At least he is polite*, she thought.

"I need to talk to someone," she said haltingly.

"What about?" He sounded less friendly, more business-like.

She shifted her weight realizing she'd not thought this out well. "Uh, I need to talk to someone about my S.I.N."

He looked puzzled for a moment. "We don't fix that here, Ma'am. You have to go to the Government Commerce Center for that. They will fill out the paperwork and file it with us later."

"Oh, no. You don't understand. I don't have a S.I.N. That's my problem. I need to talk to someone about getting one."

"Wait here." He turned to his phone and beeped someone in another office. She couldn't hear what he said, but noticed he kept glancing towards her. Victoria's heartbeat increased and her palms began to sweat. It was too late to turn back now.

The man stood up. "Follow me, please."

Victoria didn't like the impersonal and emotionless tone of the young officer's voice. She wondered if he knew who she was, after all, the police had been looking for her most of the night.

He led her to a small office at the end of a long narrow hallway. The door sign read:

INSPECTOR'S OFFICE

BUREAU OF CONSUMER TRADE

CHIEF DETECTIVE HENRY O'DONNELL

It looked so formal. Victoria gulped, wondering if she was about to meet these mysterious "THEY" who were the enemy Orpine worried so much about.

The young officer turned to her. "Henry will help you," he said, turning in a military style and heading back to his desk down the hall.

She watched him walk away and stood awkwardly inside the doorway for a moment until Henry looked up. He motioned to her to sit down in the chair in front of his desk. She concluded Henry had just arrived. He was organizing his desk and putting away his lunch in the bottom drawer. *Maybe he hasn't heard about the warehouse yet.* She felt hopeful.

"I didn't catch your name?" Henry said.

"Victoria."

He nodded. "Just Victoria?"

"For now, if you don't mind. Just Victoria."

"You have a problem with your S.I.N.?"

She nodded uneasily.

"You can have it checked at any Commerce Center you know. They are trained to correct any irregularities. What happened? Did you damage it somehow?"

"No. I, uh, well, you see," she paused.

Henry was fortyish she thought, a little heavy set with receding hair which was neatly combed. He looks kind, she concluded. She hoped. At least he looks kinder that that B.C.T. agent back at the convenience store.

"Victoria, could you get to the point. We are very busy here this morning. I've got a lot of activity from the night to investigate."

She swallowed hard. *Maybe this wasn't such a good idea.* The clock on the wall behind Henry showed 7:15. It occurred to her that every moment that passed she was letting Orpine down. "I have no S.I.N."

Henry stared at her for a long moment. "What?"

She cleared her throat. "I have no S.I.N."

"Everyone has a S.I.N." he stated.

She shook her head. "I don't. Never have."

"Never?"

"No. Can you help me?"

He thought for a moment, then got up and closed the door to his office. He sat back down behind his desk. "Go on. Explain to me how it is that you come to have no S.I.N. Start at the beginning. Don't leave anything out. I want to hear this. I need to know everything if I'm to help you."

Victoria sat up straight in the chair and looked him in the eye. "My husband and I have been living up north in the Allagash for nearly seven years. We leased property from the Paper Company. I haven't been back here since we left, and I didn't know about the currency changes until I got here a few days ago.

My husband is a Vet from the Euro/Asia War. He has R.I.T.S. and needs Trioxin. He was gravely ill when I left, too ill to travel. Up to now he was able to get his medicine from The Wilderness Store, but it burned down last week. He's all out. I've tried everything to get his prescription filled but haven't been successful. I'm not trying to break any laws. I'm desperate. Please, can you help me?"

"You're the one who escaped from the store on Wednesday?"

She nodded.

He looked at her intently.

"I cut my hair," she said.

"Oh, that must be it. I didn't recognize you. You don't look like the photo." He pulled out a large black and white photo from a folder on his desk and handed it to her and smiled.

"No one else recognized you, either. You just walked right in here, bold-as-be-damned, past all these alert and observant police officers."

She smiled, too. "Will you help me?"

He frowned. "You've violated a lot of laws."

"I didn't mean to,"

"It doesn't matter. We have been given a mandate to stop all the insurgencies and enforce the new Trade System. There is zero tolerance for dissidents."

"But I told you, I'm not a dissident."

"Then why were you living in the wilderness for the past seven years?"

"My husband and I just wanted to get away from it all."

"Some people might call that dissident behavior."

"Haven't you ever wanted to get away?"

"Wanted to, yes. Did it, no."

"We didn't do anything illegal."

"Ah, well, now, that remains to be seen." He printed out a report on his computer and read it over.

"It says here you used currency or attempted to anyway. That is a felony." He glanced up at her from the paper. His expression was somber.

"You resisted arrest, assaulted an officer, broke into a warehouse and attempted to steal some regulated drugs. Then you resisted arrest again." He looked back up at her again.

Victoria grimaced. She wished she could explain, but it didn't seem like anyone was going to comprehend her predicament. She shrugged.

"You've been busy," he said.

"I'm desperate. My husband will die soon if I don't return with Trioxin. Why doesn't anyone understand that?"

"I understand that you have broken several laws. This is not minor. This is very serious. The penalties are stiff. You could go to prison for many years."

Victoria straightened in her chair and looked him directly in the eyes. "My husband is a Veteran. He contracted R.I.T.S. serving his country. Hasn't he suffered enough? He's sick and he's dying!" She choked. "If he isn't already dead," she whispered.

"Where is he? We could send someone to bring him back to the hospital for help."

She thought about this for a moment. She remembered their war games and Orpine's fear that the authorities were going to attack them someday.

"No," she said shaking her head. "I need to go back to him with the medicine. Once he's feeling better, we will both come back and explain everything."

"We can send help," Henry offered again. She sensed he was truly trying to help.

"Orpine is sick. He's feverish. In his confusion, he might not know who you are and mistakenly think you're coming after him."

"Why would he think that? You said you two haven't done anything illegal."

"He's afraid. He believes some government forces are not so benevolent."

"So he is a subversive."

"No. He's sick. He might misunderstand your intentions."

"Is he militia?"

"No. We're by ourselves. Alone. We are not militia."

"Then I don't understand why he thinks government forces are out to get him?"

How can I explain it when I don't understand it myself, she thought.

"Let me go back to him. You can arrest me if you like. I'll come back and do whatever you want. Please, just help me save my husband."

Henry sighed. "It's not that simple. I'm sorry. The only way is to send in a police force and bring him back. I assure you he'll get medical treatment."

"Why can't I just get my own S.I.N."

"The amnesty period ended last year."

"Amnesty? From what?"

"From avoiding the new Computer Trade Network, that is from what. Don't you realize that everyone must be part of the system if it is to work? It's not fair for some to do their own thing while everyone else complies."

"I don't understand any of this," Victoria cried. "What is a S.I.N. anyway?"

Henry smiled slightly. "Let me explain it to you, then. You see, there are lots of folks who don't like paying their fair share of taxes. And there are lots of folks who like to steal from other folks. You understand that, don't you?"

She nodded.

"Well, the government had to find a way to control all these illegal activities. A critical point had been reached when the whole monetary system was in jeopardy. If the holes in the system weren't stopped, our federal reserve was going to fail. The IRS was no longer able to keep up with the cheaters and tax evaders." He studied her to determine if she were really getting what he was saying.

"At any rate, it was determined by law that all citizens must comply with the rules of the Consumer Trade Network. There was plenty of warning so people could turn in their hidden currency. You know, all those people who kept money under their mattresses." He laughed.

She smiled patiently.

"We have a very sophisticated system to identify people. You'll see when we put you through the tests."

"Tests?"

"It takes three matches for a positive ID. Hand (he held up his hand) for fingerprints; Eye (He pointed to his right eye) for optical scanning; and Voice (he nodded) for vocal patterns. These are entered into the main computer and made available to Law Enforcement universally. U.A.I., that the technical term. Universal Availability Identification.

"But what is a S.I.N.?" Victoria asked again.

"Ah, that's the implant. It contains all this information and more and is read by the universal scanners. It has your State Identification Number which is similar to the social security numbers used in the past, but it is expanded to include such things as your banking account number, medical history, purchasing history, and stuff like that. It enables you to transfer debits and credit on your personal credit ledger in the Universal Monetary System. No more currency. Everything is done on the Consumer Trade Network."

"E-Cash?" Victoria remembered the term for electronic purchasing from years ago.

Henry smiled. "Call it what you like: Cyber-currency, Funny Money, Digital Dollars. It doesn't matter because it's all the same. It's all one huge banking network that keeps an accounting of every single transaction we do."

"One system? You mean there's only one bank?"

He nodded. "The Consumer Trade Network absorbed all the monetary institutions. That was the only way it could work and the only way to prevent DIGI-Crimes and counterfeit systems. There have to be controls in a centralized system to avoid fraud and scams. All transactions must go through one central system."

"It all sounds like a good idea unless you're in my situation."

"It's more than a good idea," Henry said. "Think of the savings. No more currency and no more printing costs or special paper. No more armed guards or armored trucks to transport money. No more bank tellers counting money. The savings in time and personnel are enormous. Not to mention the savings in paperwork. Taxes are filed instantly at the end of each month and adjusted at the end of the year. Taxpayers save millions, too. There are even fewer lobbyists in Washington now!"

"I wonder if all those people are happy to be out of a job," Victoria said.

Henry smiled. "Even the horse and buggy went by the wayside to progress. Everyone has to adopt to changes."

"Or get left behind," she said.

"Well, times change. People have to change with them."

"Why an implant with all this other technology?"

"Just think for a moment. You never have to worry about being robbed or forgetting to bring money or credit cards with you when you go out. You can't lose an implant."

"And the government gets to know everything about me. Don't people lose their privacy with this new Trade Network? Doesn't that worry you?"

"Believe me, what is lost is more than offset by what is gained. The benefits of the new system outweigh privacy concerns. I'll gladly sacrifice some privacy for safety and convenience, tax savings and less crime."

"If there's no more crime then why do you still have a job?"

"We got a new kind of criminal today. They are not motivated by greed so much as by fear and misinformation," he said.

"When did fear and misunderstanding become a crime?" she said.

"It is if it leads to breaking the law," he said.

"Maybe society's psyche hasn't caught up to technology," she suggested.

"Smart observation. It is primitive behavior to be afraid of what you don't yet comprehend."

"It may be primitive, but it's common human behavior," she said, remembering her friends back in the Allagash.

"That's what leads to irrational and superstitious beliefs on the part of some, especially ignorant and fringe people."

"It could be healthy skepticism," she said.

Henry eyed her curiously. "If they'd just be realistic, they'd understand it's for everyone's good, even theirs."

"Maybe," she said, "but why is it implanted?"

"It's the most practical and cost-effective method of personal identification."

"Sounds like a government branding, like people are herds of livestock," she said.

"Branding?" he asked.

"You know, like a farmer brands his animals so he knows where they are and doesn't lose any."

"Guess you could look at it that way, but it's not all bad. For instance, suppose a child is missing. It used to be horrible to search for a missing child. Now we can locate them almost instantly. It's already saved many children, and their anxious parents."

"I suppose that's good," Victoria conceded.

"Darn right that's good. You'd think so, too, if you'd ever had to comfort anguished parents."

"Can we find out all that information the government has recorded about us?" she asked.

"It's not necessary for you to know everything," he said, shifting his position in his chair. "Let's just say it's impossible for anyone to just disappear anymore. There's always a trail. Let's just leave it at that."

"Uh, huh," she said, doubtfully.

"And crime is practically nil," he said a little defensively. "Why would anyone steal when they can't sell it on the open market? No more bribery, kidnapping or extortion. No more cheating on income taxes. That alone saves the government (he pointed at her) and you taxpayers billions of dollars a year. That's big taxpayer savings, mind you. Before the new system, we used to have to make up all that lost revenue by increasing taxes on the honest folks. Honest folks appreciate the fact that we'll be able to reduce taxes once everyone is online and when everyone conforms and pays their share of taxes. That's why it's essential everyone conforms. You can see that, can't you?"

"Yes. I can see what you're saying, but I'm not a criminal. How do you explain my situation? I didn't know about all these changes. Why do you have to make it so hard for someone like me who isn't a real threat to your system?"

"Anyone who doesn't conform IS a threat. That's just it. Whether they intend to be or not, they threaten the system. Unfortunately, a few always spoil it for the rest of us."

She sighed.

"Now, let's get you positively identified, shall we?" He stood up after pulling restraints out of his desk drawer.

"You're going to handcuff me?"

He came around the desk and stood in front of her. She stood up.

"I came here on my own and turned myself in."

Henry looked at her. She wondered was that pity she saw in his eyes?

"Regulations," he said, shrugging.

"I'm not going to run away now. Where would I go? Why are you treating me this way?"

"I have to follow procedure."

"I'm not a criminal," she repeated, lips trembling.

"All right," he said, putting the restraints on his desk.

He took her arm firmly, "this way."

Victoria followed him to an elevator. They went down to the basement level and when the elevator door opened, a maze of corridors was before them. He led her to a lab where a technician looked up as they entered.

"Morning, Henry. Early start today, huh?"

"Morning Liz. Need a positive ID on her. Can you do it now?"

"Where is her booking paperwork?"

"Not ready yet."

"Come back when it is ready."

"Liz, I need a positive ID first," Henry said firmly.

The technician studied Victoria for a moment. "Okay, Henry. For you I'll do it, but you'll owe me."

Henry smiled. "How's dinner Friday night sound?"

Liz smiled. "Sounds good, Henry. Our usual place?"

He nodded and released Victoria's arm.

Liz motioned to Victoria. "Sit here." It was a large chair like the dentist uses. Victoria sat down timidly. Liz adjusted the height of the seat and put a machine in front of Victoria's face.

"Put your chin on that rest, please, and look straight ahead."

Victoria complied and the machine clicked. A bright light flashed and the technician reached over and pulled the machine back.

"Be ready in an hour," she said to Henry.

"Thanks, Liz. Can you send it to my office?"

She nodded. "Sure. Don't forget the paperwork."

Henry led Victoria to another lab where several white-robed technicians were talking. "They're just going to take a blood sample for the DNA Bank," he whispered to her, giving her a re-assuring pat on her arm.

She thought this seemed more like a hospital than a police station. How much things had changed in so short of a time. *Have we been gone that long?*

After the sample was drawn a young man began setting up a soundproof booth. "You'll need to sit inside and when I tell you, say the words on the screen.

Speak into the microphone."

She did as instructed, reading first the alphabet, then several words that seemed to include a spectrum of vocal sounds.

Henry and Victoria returned to the elevator. "Now, we'll know exactly who you are," Henry said as the doors closed.

"Will I be able to get my own S.I.N. now?"

Henry looked away. "That will require a court order."

"How long will that take?"

He sighed and didn't answer. The elevator doors opened on the third floor. She looked around. Guards stood on each corner of the elevator opening. She swallowed hard realizing it was the holding area.

Henry took her arm securely and they stepped out of the elevator. She turned back towards the doors.

"No you don't," he said, holding her securely. A guard stepped forward to assist.

Tears flooded her eyes. "My husband is dying! I can't stay here. I have to get back to him. I thought you were going to help me."

He frowned and motioned to the officer to take her. "I'll make this as quick as I can, I assure you, but it'll only take longer if you resist. You've already made matters worse for yourself."

Two large guards now stood beside Victoria, one holding each of her arms.

"Please don't do this," she whispered to Henry.

They pulled her away as the elevator doors closed and Henry was gone.

"Let me go! Let me go!" she cried, struggling. They pulled her to a holding cell and pushed her down inside. Before she could get back up, the door was shut and locked.

The guards wiped their hands.

"Cling-on!" one said as he turned away.

"NOOOOOO!" Victoria wailed. "Let me out of here!"

Three hours later the two guards returned. "Come with us," one commanded. Her wrists were secured in front of her and she was escorted back to Henry's office. He nodded for her to sit down.

"Untie her hands," he ordered. The guard did so reluctantly.

"Leave us." Henry nodded towards his door.

"Wait outside."

The guard gave Victoria a look of disdain and left. Henry turned to her. "I'm sorry you had to be arrested. I believe you are sincere."

She looked away. It wasn't her detainment that made her upset. It was Orpine. Time was running out; she could sense it. She feared he was already dead and that she had let him down. She choked back a sob. *Maybe Orpine was right. Maybe I was a fool to come back and trust the authorities again.*

"We have your positive identification: Victoria Karen Stuart Alexander Wilderbee, born January 4, 2009, in Berlin, NH-Victoria Karen Stuart. You disappeared seven years ago and there's been no evidence of any activity on your part since. It's as if you disappeared off the face of the earth."

She listened patiently wondering if he was going to help her obtain the needed S.I.N. so she could save Orpine.

"Fits your story," Henry said with a grin. He looked back at the folder in front of him.

"You first married David Alexander in June 2029. Says you had a daughter, Colleen, born in 2030 and deceased 2038."

My God, he knows everything about me, she thought. "She was only five," Victoria said. "I suppose you know how she died?"

Henry nodded his head. "Cancer."

"Cancer caused by pollution, covered up by government agencies. Doesn't your report say that? Did your report forget to mention the Crystal Swamp incident?" She could hear the bitterness in her voice, but she didn't care anymore. Henry could think whatever he wanted.

"I'm sorry," he said. "It isn't in here, but I'm sure it's just an oversight."

"Yeah, an oversight. That's a typical bureaucratic answer."

Henry returned to his folder and read on. "You and David divorced in 2035."

Victoria recalled that awful time in her life and how she'd been certain there would never be a happy moment for her again. She had truly believed that and Henry was bringing back the pain without realizing it.

"Losing a child often causes stress in a marriage," Henry said.

Lots of people told me that back then, Victoria thought, *but I know the real reason. David blamed me for Colleen's death. He never said so, but I know he did. And he could never forgive me. I could never forgive me.*

"You married Orpine Jon Wilderbee on January 4th, 2037." He glanced at her. "Your birthday?"

"We decided it would be easier to celebrate two things at once, my birthday and our anniversary," she said.

He smiled. "Wish I'd thought of that." He looked back down at the papers. "Orpine was born on August 20, 2003, in Standish, Maine, and served in the Euro-Asia war for three years from 2030 to 2033. Says here he received a medical discharge."

"He was wounded and sent home. A year later he was diagnosed with R.I.T.S," Victoria said.

"The FBI file says you were an adamant government protestor."

"A protestor?" Victoria looked surprised.

"That's what it says."

"I was never a protestor."

"Says you were."

"When?"

"Before you disappeared. From the time your daughter died, 2034, until 2037. Got any idea why they might think that about you?"

"I wasn't a protestor," Victoria said. "No one ever accused me of that. I was the one trying to tell everyone that they were over-reacting."

"Says you sued the United States Government," Henry glanced up at her.

"So did everyone else in the Crystal Swamp Project. What does that have to do with now? The government admitted they were wrong and settled the lawsuit out of court. I wasn't the only one suing because it was a class action suit. My daughter died because of a government cover up. They admitted it in the end. How does that make me a protestor?"

"Doesn't say anything about a settlement. Only that you were considered a danger and the FBI put you on a watch list. Your emotional profile indicates possible subversive activities."

"I don't believe this," Victoria cried.

"Would you like to tell me what you've been doing for the past seven years and with whom you've been associating?"

He turned on a small recorder.

"I've already told you everything. Orpine and I live alone in the Allagash wilderness. That's all. There's no subversive activity. We aren't a threat to anyone."

He looked at her.

"I don't have to answer any more questions," she said. "Don't I have a right to a lawyer?"

"You do," Henry nodded. "We can do this later if you wish, after your lawyer arrives. I trust you have one retained, but wonder how you would have paid for legal services?"

"I don't have a lawyer."

Henry turned off the recorder. "Look, I believe you're sincere. Make it easier for yourself and just answer the questions. Tell us everything and I'll do all I can to help you." He put the recorder back on.

"There's nothing more to tell you."

"You don't seem to grasp the gravity of your situation," he said sternly.

"All I understand is that my husband is dying. Nothing else matters. You said you'd help me, and now I'm being accused of things that I've never done. I don't know how to get my own S.I.N. or I'd have done so. What do you want from me? Do you want my money? You can have all of it. Everything. I just need Trioxin for Orpine. Even just a little so he can recover enough to come back for treatment."

"You have money? Real currency?"

She clenched her jaw. *Doesn't he hear anything I'm saying?*

Henry's door opened and an officer looked inside. "Henry, got a minute?" he said.

"Sure. You wait here. I'll be right back."

Victoria looked around Henry's office. There were several citations framed on the walls and a large group photo of officers, probably his graduating class she surmised. A large portrait hung on the wall behind his desk and she realized it was the President of the United States, but she had no idea who the man was. *How did I get so out of touch?* She wondered.

She glanced at the folder on Henry's desk, the one that contained her photo and all that information. She glanced behind her at the open door, then reached for it and turned it around and began examining it.

Several pages contained details of her recent encounters with the authorities. There were several photos from the convenience store and even some from the warehouse.

She moved the papers aside and noticed another folder underneath. Inside was a packet that contained a small silver computer disk. On the outside of the disk was a spider web design. The accompanying report listed several computer viruses and she realized she'd opened someone else's file and started to put it back.

Someone walked past the open doorway startling Victoria and she dropped the disk. She reached for it and the folders spilled onto the floor. Frantically, she gathered the papers back and put them inside the folders. Then she saw the disk on the floor and reached for it, again startled by a person walking past the door. She slipped the disk absent- mindedly into her jacket pocket and stood up.

Victoria crept towards the open office door and peeked outside. Henry was down the hall talking to another officer and a female guard. She pulled her head back inside Henry's office just as they looked her way. They didn't notice her.

It was a mistake to come here. They're not going to help me. Not in time to save Orpine, she thought. *I have to get out of here!*

She glanced back outside and waited until Henry turned aside, then walked slowly down the hallway trying to be inconspicuous.

In the reception area she passed by the officer who had originally greeted her early that morning. Victoria smiled at the officer who just watched as she passed by, then he turned to answer the phone.

The clock on the wall read 11:30am. Victoria felt the time draining away as she opened the door and slipped outside. Restraining herself from running, she walked past several people coming inside and several police officers.

She kept her eyes down hoping they wouldn't recognize her, hoping they all assumed the hunt was over since she'd turned herself in. She crossed the street and walked past the shop and around the corners, then jogged until she came to a small park.

There was a fountain with four benches circled around it. Victoria sat down on one and pulled her knees to her chest, watching the water, thinking.

She sniffed the cool morning air and wiped away a tear. It was Friday. Orpine would be very bad now and time was running out, if it wasn't already too late. She visualized the calendar she'd X'd, knowing she'd let her husband down. She was supposed to be back by now. She'd promised.

After a while exhaustion overcame her and she rested her head on her knees and briefly dozed. The warm sun melted away the chill she'd felt and when she opened her eyes, the area was transformed into a bright cheerful intersection with pedestrians hurrying in the noon hour.

"Mind if I sit here?"

Victoria looked up towards the sun and squinted at the silhouette of a young woman.

"Sure," she said, drawing her legs back to her side.

"Be my guest."

The young woman smiled and Victoria thought she looked familiar somehow, like someone she'd known in the distant past, but upon closer inspection, she decided it was just a similarity. She'd never met this person before.

"You're not from around these parts, are you?"

Victoria shifted uneasily. "No, just visiting."

The woman smiled. "No offence, but it looks like you've been outside a long time. Did you sleep on this bench last night? I'm surprised you weren't rounded up and taken to the shelter."

Victoria looked around discreetly for an escape route, just in case, suddenly feeling quite vulnerable.

"Hey, I didn't mean to scare you. I'm Becki. I have lots of friends who don't conform. It's no big deal to me. I'll just go on my way now. I'm sorry I bothered you."

The woman stood up and started walking away.

"Wait," Victoria called.

The woman turned around and grinned. "I knew it. I can spot you guys a mile away."

"You're right," Victoria said. "I am new at this. I could use a friend. Can we start over?"

Becki quickly returned to the bench and sat down eager to learn more. Victoria noticed her deep blue- green eyes and her blonde hair. She smiled, thinking Becki was a communer--no question about it, she fit the profile.

"Actually, I'm not alone," Victoria said.

Becki looked surprised.

"I came with someone who was supposed to wait for me. Jerk! He left me stranded. I never should have trusted him." Victoria studied Becki's response but couldn't detect anything positive or negative.

"Maybe I can help. I know lots of people back at the retreat. They're usually very helpful."

"Retreat?" Victoria thought, I was right--she's a communer.

"I'm going there now. Why don't you come with me?"

Becki took Victoria to a remote farmhouse just outside Woodinville in the direction Victoria had come that night, past the Regional Government Processing Center.

When they got on the public transit, Becki paid both fares with her own S.I.N., not asking Victoria, but assuming.

Victoria had a lot of questions for Becki but decided to wait until later to ask them. They rode silently.

The farmhouse was big with several built-on additions and a huge dining area. People were working everywhere, some painting, some gardening, others cleaning, chopping wood, or cooking. Several loaves of fresh bread cooled on a large counter and Victoria eyed it enviously as they passed. Becki noticed and laughed.

"Hi, Sal. This here's my new friend, Victoria. I think she's hungry."

Victoria smiled at the man.

"Didn't have breakfast, huh?" the round, white- aproned, jovial man asked.

"No. And no dinner either, now that I think about it."

"You sit yourself right down there at the breakfast bar. I'll have some dandy little eats for you in a jiffy. No one goes hungry around here."

Victoria ate ravenously, surprised at her appetite. She smiled gratefully to Sal who watched with pride.

"Thanks," she said. "This really hit the spot."

Sal smiled broadly. He loved making people happy with his cooking and Victoria had just made his day.

Becki left while Victoria ate and now returned. "Come with me. I'll show you your room."

"My room?"

"Yes. You're going to share my room if that's okay?"

"But I can't," Victoria said.

"Of course you can," Becki said.

"No, I can't stay here," Victoria said.

"Well how do you expect to go anywhere?" Becki asked and Victoria knew she was referring to her inability to pay her bus fare.

"I appreciate the offer, but I really do have to leave."

"We'll discuss that later. First, follow me. You need to rest and clean up."

Victoria followed Becki upstairs to the third floor and a small bedroom with two bunks wedged between the slanted walls. "I got the bottom bunk," Becki said, "since I was here first."

"That's fine with me. I like the top bunk," Victoria said feeling a little nervous. This tiny room felt all too confining.

"What's the matter?" Becki asked.

"I really can't stay here," Victoria said, sitting down behind a small desk.

Becki sat on her bunk. "Why not?"

"I have to get back to Orpine, my husband."

"Where is he?"

"North. He's sick. R.I.T.S. I have to get him some Trioxin soon or he'll die." She looked down sadly not saying that she really feared he was already dead. Worse, that she feared she'd let him die all alone--that she'd failed him just like she failed her daughter Colleen. A tear rolled down her cheek and she quickly brushed it away.

"You don't have a S.I.N., do you?" Becki asked.

"You noticed. That's why you paid the bus fare."

She nodded. "You're not that hard to spot, truthfully. I'm surprised you got this far. Must be others have helped you?"

Victoria felt uneasy with Becki's questions.

Becki grinned and Victoria forced herself to return a smile.

"Not really. Like you said, I've been lucky. But not lucky enough. I still haven't got Orpine's Trioxin."

"That's easy enough," Becki announced.

"Easy?" Victoria looked at Becki incredulously. How could this young woman think obtaining Trioxin was easy?

"Yeah. I know exactly where you can get it. I'll help you."

"Really?" Victoria brightened.

"Sure. There's a bit of a risk, but you can handle it."

Victoria nodded. "Let's go now. I really need to hurry."

"I just have to make one phone call. You wait here. I'll be right back. Don't worry. We'll get your husband's Trioxin to him."

"Thanks, Becki," Victoria said.

"Don't give it a thought. I like taking control and solving situations." She smiled and went out the door.

Victoria felt a twinge of uncertainly but couldn't figure out why. Maybe it just seemed too easy after all she'd been through trying to obtain the medicine. *I must be tired*, she decided. *Things will look clearer when I rested.*

She went to the dormer window and watched the people working below. *Nice place*, she thought. *Maybe Orpine and I should come here when he's well. We've been living alone too long.*

Victoria waited for what seemed like a long time and decided to go downstairs to find Becki. Perhaps she'd been detained somewhere, or forgotten she'd left her in the bedroom.

People were busy inside the old farmhouse, some cleaning and dusting. In one room several people were painting the walls. Outside various farm chores were being done, women were harvesting strawberries from a garden, and delicious smells wafted from the kitchen.

Victoria was uncertain where she should go and what she should do, so she went into the library and began browsing through the books on the shelves.

An older woman returned a book to a shelf near Victoria and smiled at her. "I haven't seen you before?"

"No. I'm just visiting. Becki brought me here."

"Oh. Where is Becki?"

"She's gone on an errand," Victoria said. She thought for a moment, then asked, "How long has Becki lived here?"

"Becki doesn't actually live here. She visits often, though," the woman answered.

"She isn't a member?" Victoria asked.

The woman laughed. "Well, I think she's a little more than a member. She owns this place."

"She does?"

"Yes," the woman nodded. "She opened it to us a couple years ago. We're glad she did. Before that we traveled around and lived in tent communities. Here we can raise our own organically grown food. It's so much nicer. And Becki helped us all go legal, too. Those that weren't already legal." The woman blushed a little.

"Sounds like you all compromised," Victoria said.

The woman considered this for a moment, then nodded. "I guess you could say that. We gave up some of our freedoms, but we get to do what we want. Some think that's why the new welfare credits were established, to force people to settle down."

"So they can keep tabs on you," Victoria said.

"Excuse me," the woman said and left.

Victoria turned back to the shelf. She looked around the room. No one else remained in the library, so she sat down at a large desk that had a computer on it. A moment after she sat down, the computer beeped.

"Hello," it said, startling her.

She typed: HELLO

"What's your name?" the computer asked.

VICTORIA. WHAT'S YOURS?

"It's a mystery," the computer said.

Victoria smiled. *Probably some lonely kid playing on the Internet.*

She typed: WHY ARE YOU USING VOICE SIMULATION? WHY DON'T YOU USE YOUR OWN VOICE OR TYPE THE WORDS?

Instantly the computer answered. "Harder for them to catch me. No voice print, no words to read. They'd have to be listening to me."

OH, I SEE. She shifted in her seat.

"Who are you looking for?" the computer asked.

Victoria thought for a moment, then pulled the small computer disk out of her pocket, the one she'd taken from the police station. She slipped it into the slot and it started humming.

She typed: I'M LOOKING FOR SPIDER WEB.

"Wrong," the computer said.

WHY?

"Too long. Only one name."

WELL, HOW ABOUT SPIDER?

There was a long silence and Victoria figured the person had tired of the game. She started to stand up.

"Spider wants to know who's asking?"

She looked at the screen and sat back down and typed: VICTORIA

"Victoria who?"

JUST VICTORIA. ONLY ONE NAME, REMEMBER?

"Spider wants to know why you want him?"

Victoria's stomach churned. Perhaps this wasn't smart. His name was in a police file after all. She glanced around to make sure she was alone.

She typed: I WANT TO KNOW ABOUT THE VIRUS.

"No exposure." The computer answered instantly as if it knew her questions before she finished typing them.

WHAT DOES THAT MEAN?

"Can't catch a virus if you're not exposed to one."

I'M TALKING ABOUT A COMPUTER VIRUS, Victoria typed.

"No exposure. It doesn't work without exposure."

She thought for a moment, then typed: WHAT IF YOU COULD GET EXPOSURE?

"Spider says if you can get him exposure, he can get the virus injected. It requires direct exposure."

WELL, MR SPIDER, WHOEVER YOU ARE, I THINK YOU WEAVE A COMPLICATED WEB. IF I EVER NEED YOU, HOW DO I REACH YOU?

"Connect to the World Wide Web, and insert the disc, ask for Spider like you just did. If you get me into the mainframe, I'll tell you how to execute the virus."

WHY DO I FEEL LIKE I JUST COMMITTED A FELONY?

"Because you did!"

The screen went blank. Victoria stared at the video screen for a moment, then removed the disk and it back into her pocket. *Hackers*, she thought, *they just can't resist the challenge.*

Becki came back twenty minutes later and found Victoria in the library.

"It's all set," she said. "I found the Trioxin for you."

Victoria looked at her. "All set. How did you do it?"

"We're going to see old Doc Roberts. He helps vets like your husband all the time. Come on. We'll take my truck."

They bounced along the roads for several miles before turning onto a main road again, then heading towards another village. Becki stopped in front of a small medical facility. "You wait here. I'll be right back," Becki ordered.

Ten minutes later she returned and handed Victoria a prescription jar full of Trioxin.

Victoria gasped. "How did you do that?"

Becki smiled slyly. "Can't give away my secrets. Let's just say I have connections."

It was late afternoon when they returned to the farmhouse. "We'll leave first thing in the morning," Becki said.

"We?" Victoria asked. "I think I should go alone. It might be dangerous. Besides, I want to go right now, not in the morning. There's no time to waste. I can't wait until tomorrow."

"Nonsense. I'm coming with you and we're leaving at first light."

"But I really should go tonight," Victoria protested, uneasy with the power Becki seemed to wield over her.

"No way. I've got everything under control," Becki stated. "Look at you. You're a wreck. A good night's sleep will do wonders. Besides, I'm hungry. Sal's got a nice dinner planned in your honor. You don't want to disappoint Sal, do you?"

"But you don't understand. I have to leave now!"

"And how do you plan to get there? My vehicle isn't going anywhere until tomorrow morning." Becky spoke with confidence.

Victoria realized she was correct, and didn't want to jeopardize use of a vehicle to get back to Orpine. She'd make no better time walking, that was for sure. Reluctantly, she agreed. "Okay, Becki. First thing tomorrow."

"When the rooster crows," Becki said, grinning.

As they turned into the driveway, Victoria noticed an old car parked near the barn. "Whose car is that?" she asked.

"Which one?" Becki asked.

"That one!" Victoria jumped out of Becki's truck before it had come to a complete stop and ran over to the car.

"Mel! You son-of-a-bitch!"

Becki ran over to her. "What is it Victoria?"

"Where is he? Where is that slime? I could kill him!"

"Mel? You know Mel?"

Victoria fumed. "Unfortunately, yes." She spotted him going inside and ran after him.

"There you are!"

His eyes widened. "Look. I can explain everything," he said, holding up his hands as she was about to attack him. "Stop."

"You left me there! I told you to wait."

"The cops came. They told me to move one. What was I supposed to do? I came back later, but you weren't there. Hell, that place was crawling with police. I had to get out!"

"You're a jerk, Mel. A royal jerk! You're an insult to the Vets. How can anyone trust you? Look at yourself. You're pathetic. A pathetic druggie!"

"Hey, I came back for you, but you were gone. What was I supposed to do?"

"Save it for someone who cares. Give me back my locket!"

He pulled it out of his pocket and handed it towards her. She grabbed it and shook her head as she passed by him. "Jerk!"

"I'm sorry."

"Sure you are. You're a sorry excuse for a man."

Becki eyed Mel as she passed him and hurried to catch up to Victoria. "So, someone did help you along the way," she whispered to her as they entered the dining room.

"Our guests have arrived," Sal announced, anxious to please Victoria once more with his fine cuisine.

"Here, sit right here, pretty lady."

"Victoria, it is you," a young woman said from across the large table.

"Coralee. You're all right," Victoria said, surprised but pleased to see her. "Your mom and dad are worried about you."

"Well, you can tell them for me that I'm just fine and happy to be here. And I'm never going back. I don't care if I never see another tote road in my life."

"You two know each other?" Becki sat down beside Coralee.

"She's the one who squealed on me," Coralee said.

"Coralee, you know that's not fair," Victoria said.

Before anything else could be said, Sal brought in his masterpiece, a standing rib roast. Everyone complimented him.

Victoria looked at Becki as she ate opposite her and wondered about her reaction to Mel helping her at the Medical Distribution Center. *I have to trust her*, Victoria thought.

She felt the jar of Trioxin inside her pocket, just to affirm that it was really there. She smiled. *Becki helped me get the Trioxin. I don't know how she did it. But she helped me. I have to trust her. I have to. I have no other choice.*

Victoria replaced her locket around her neck. Mel sat way at the end of the dining table and sheepishly picked at his food, much to Sal's disappointment.

Becki smiled at Victoria from across the table.

I have to trust her.

Chapter 10

Almost There

It was still dark when Victoria climbed down from the bunk. To her surprise, Becki was already up and her bed neatly made. She quickly pulled on her pants and shirt and grabbed her jacket, checking to make sure the Trioxin was still there. It was.

Downstairs, Becki had made coffee and handed her a cup. "Cream and sugar," Becki said. "I figured you drank it that way."

"Sounds good," Victoria said, anxious to get going. It was Friday, July 1st and she was now two days late returning. She hoped she wasn't too late. She prayed she wasn't.

"Aren't you glad we stayed the night?" Becki asked, sipping her coffee. "I told you that you needed to sleep. You sure did, too. I had to get up because you snored so loud."

Victoria smiled weakly, doubting that she snored. She wondered if Becki even slept in her bed. She'd gone to sleep before Becki came into the room. *What a stupid thing to think about*, Victoria thought. *Who cares where Becki slept?*

"We should get going," Victoria said.

"In a minute. I want to put some lunch in the cooler. Got a feeling it's going to be a long day," Becki said.

Two cars drove into the driveway. Their headlights shone onto the porch.

"Who's that?" Victoria asked, at the same instant a knot formed in the pit of her stomach. One of the cars had a flashing blue light, angrily slicing through the pre-dawn darkness.

"Shit!" Becki said. "What do they want?"

Coralee stood in the kitchen doorway. Victoria glanced at her and knew she'd turned her in.

"Why?" she asked.

Coralee sniffed but didn't answer.

"Hurry!   Come with me," Becki said, grabbing Victoria's arm.

They ran out the back door and into the big barn just as the front door opened. Victoria heard Coralee. "They went that way. Out back!"

Becki started her Land Rover inside the dark barn and put it into gear. She flicked on her front lights and buckled her seatbelt.

"Hold on!" She hit the accelerator and crashed through the door, past the police cars and onto the street. By the time the officers got back to their cars, they were out of sight. She cut through a field onto a dirt road.

"I know a shortcut," she said, grinning at Victoria who was holding onto the seat and doorknob.

A short time later, they came out of the woods and onto a main road. The sun was just peeking over the horizon. "Where are we heading?" Becki asked.

"Phalarope Landing," Victoria answered.

Becki looked surprised and glanced at Victoria who stared straight ahead at the road, deep in thought. *I can't believe Coralee hates me so much as to turn me in to the police*. Maybe I was wrong to tell Ralph and Judy about her drug use. Maybe I should have just minded my own business. That's probably what Orpine would have told me. If only I could have asked him. I was so sure it was the right thing to do, just like so many other times in my life, and it backfired.

An hour later they drove through the center of Phalarope Landing and Becki slowed down.

"Where?"

"Keep going, down that road," Victoria pointed. Victoria noticed a vehicle that had been behind them for a while. She watched it from the passenger side mirror.

"What's wrong?" Becki asked.

"I think we're being followed," Victoria said.

"No. It can't be."

"That car behind us has been going our same way since we left Woodinville. They even followed us down this old road."

"Nonsense," Becki said confidently. "No one is following us. You're just getting paranoid. There are only a few roads to travel. Where else would they go?"

As they passed Walter and Val's old farmhouse, Victoria looked to see if they were around. The vehicle behind them turned into their driveway. Victoria watched in the mirror as two people got out and headed towards the front door.

"Know those folks?" Becki asked.

"I don't know anyone here," Victoria lied.

They rounded a corner and out of sight.

"Mel is from this area," Becki said.

Victoria didn't acknowledge her comment. "Keep going this way."

She pulled out a map to see how to connect to her vehicle she'd left on the other side of the woods. The road wound around in that direction. She put the map down and watched the countryside.

"You're awful quiet," Becki said.

"I'm worried."

"Your husband?"

"Yes."

"Don't worry. We'll get there."

"I just hope we get there in time."

A few minutes later they passed a woman and two children walking on the side of the road not far from the Welcome to Phalarope Landing sign.

"Stop the car," Victoria said.

"What?"

"Stop the car!"

Victoria jumped out and ran over to them.

"Victoria!" Marelle exclaimed.

"Marelle, what are you doing out here?"

"I left."

"You left the commune? Why?"

"Master didn't give his permission for Danny and me to marry." Marelle sniffed, choking back a sob, and started walking, holding Robin's hand.

"Wait," Victoria said. "He could change his mind. Why are you leaving the group? I thought that was your home."

Marelle stopped and looked Victoria in the eye. She pressed her lips together tightly as if strained to say the words. "Master picked someone else for Danny." She started to walk on.

"Wait. Where are you going?"

Marelle shrugged. "I don't know. As far away as I can. You were right, Victoria. I should have listened to you. It's up to me to decide what to do with my life, not some guru!"

"Come with me," Victoria offered.

"Where are you going?"

"Back to Orpine. I got his Trioxin. After that, I can take you someplace else if you want. Or you can stay with us for a while until you decide what you want to do. You're too upset to decide now."

"I don't have any place to go," Marelle said. "And I have no more credit. Master used mine all up."

"That's okay. I don't have any credit, either. All I have is useless paper money!" Victoria smiled and Marelle brightened.

"I can't impose on you. You have your own problems. Victoria pulled the amulet out of the lining in her jacket and held it out towards Marelle, in the palm of her hand.

"We're connected, remember?" Marelle smiled.

"You helped me. Now let me help you," Victoria said.

"Are you sure we won't be a burden?"

"I'm sure. Come on."

Becki backed up the vehicle, got out and came over to them. "Do you know these folks, Victoria?" She eyed Marelle and the children. Robin clung closely to her mother. "You live around here?"

"This is my friend, Marelle, and her daughter, Robin, and her son, Jeremy. They're coming with us."

"Great," Beck said unenthusiastically, "they can sit in the back."

Everyone piled in and they continued on their way. "We need to stop up ahead," Victoria said, pointing to the dirt trail where she had ditched her jeep four days earlier.

"Why?" Becki asked.

"My jeep."

"It's not there," Marelle said, leaning forward from the back seat.

"It's not? Where is it?" Victoria asked.

"They took it the day after you left the commune."

"The police took my jeep?"

She nodded. "B.C.T."

"Of course," Becki said, "they wouldn't have just left it there. B.C.T. have the authority to confiscate any personal property from suspected currency frauds."

Victoria looked at Becki, puzzled. "Suspected? You mean they don't even have to wait for a trial? I thought people were presumed innocent until proven guilty."

Marelle laughed. "Where have you been?"

Becki smiled, too. "It's too important a crime to wait. They have to protect the integrity of the system or they'll be too much harm done to society. It all gets sorted out in the trial anyway."

"Harm? What harm?"

"Where have you been Victoria?" There was sarcasm in Becki's voice. "In order for the Consumer Trade Network to operate, no one can usurp the system. Everyone must conform. Everyone must be online. Otherwise it distorts the value of everyone's currency."

"Sounds like a lot of government intrusion into people's private affairs to me," Victoria said, remembering the policeman's similar sentiments.

Becki bristled.

Victoria noticed. "Becki, if you think the new money system is so good, why are you helping me and those communers back at your farm?"

"I just think there are some good aspects," Becki said.

"Like what? Name a few."

Marelle leaned forward from the back seat to listen.

Becki said, "Like, no more tax fraud for example. And no more price gouging during disasters. Like no more illegal immigrant employees."

"Okay, I get it. But what about privacy?" Victoria asked.

"Privacy?"

"Yes. Like, I don't want everyone, including the government to know how I spend my money. With this new system, someone can know everything about me, what books I read, what food I eat, where I live and travel, everything. Where's my privacy?"

"That shouldn't be a problem. There are safeguards in the system so no one can access your account information without your authorization."

"Even the police?" Victoria asked.

Becki shrugged. "They'd only pull your file if they had a good reason."

"Well, that doesn't make me feel any better," Victoria said.

"There are laws to protect you," Becki said. "They have to have good reasons."

"I see. So there haven't been any complaints? People are really happy with this new system?"

"There's always going to be a few who complain," Becki said. "You can't please everyone. Overall, people realize they are better off as long as other people don't cheat. Cheaters take away from those who conform. That's how people feel about the new system."

"How do you know so much about the system?" Victoria asked.

"I keep up with it. That's how you know how someone might try to beat the system if you know how it works."

"You can beat the system?" Victoria asked.

"How?"

Becki cleared her throat uneasily. "I don't know how, but no system is foolproof. It's just not possible. That's why the B.C.T. was established--to make sure controls are in place and everyone is ONLINE."

"And to give more government agents a job," Victoria sniffed.

"Right," Becki said looking away from Victoria.

"Right," Victoria repeated glancing at Marelle who looked equally concerned.

"Who is she?" Marelle mouthed silently. Victoria shook her head and turned back to watching the road.

"We should gas up," Victoria said as they approached the last filling station, the one where'd she'd nearly been arrested. "I'll wait here in the car."

"How much further?" Becki asked as she got out of the vehicle.

"We'll be lucky to get there before dark," Victoria said. Becki frowned. "I better buy some food, too. Bet you kids are hungry?"

"I will come help you," Marelle said. "You two stay here with Victoria."

Robin and Jeremy looked at Victoria. "I gotta go, Mommy," Robin whined. "Me, too, Mom," Jeremy said.

"Okay. Come with me." Marelle looked apologetically at Victoria. "We'll be right back."

"That's okay," Victoria said. She waited in the Land Rover while Becki filled the tank and headed inside the store. Marelle took the children to the rest room.

Victoria smiled despite her worry as she watched Robin skipping along beside her mother. It was taking a while for them to return and she imagined Marelle interacting with her children. She remembered Colleen and sighed, holding onto her locket.

Marelle came back with her children first. "Hop in," she said.

Soon Becki returned with a bag of goodies. She passed out sandwiches and fruit juice to everyone. Then she pulled out two bags of potato chips, handing one to Marelle and one to Victoria. Victoria's was Barbecue.

"Thanks," Victoria said, smiling. "How'd you know?"

"Know what?" Becki asked.

"That I like Barbecue chips. They're my favorite."

"Lucky guess." She got inside and they headed down the road towards the Allagash.

Robin fell asleep on her mother's lap and Jeremy quietly watched the scenery, whispering to Marelle from time to time. Victoria guided Becki back, retracing the route she'd come on Monday.

Victoria sighed often, tapping nervously on the passenger side door handle. *Hang on, Orpine*, she thought. *I'll be there soon.*

She fondled the Trioxin bottle in her left jacket pocket as if it would calm her fears and renew her hope. They drove slowly through the forest on old tote roads. Victoria sighed and tapped.

"You want me to drive,' she asked Becki, impatient with her driving.

"I'm doing okay."

"You must be getting tired. You've been driving for hours."

"No. I enjoy driving. Especially in the country." Becki looked about in an over-exaggerated way.

"I really need to get there. Is there any way we could drive a little faster?" Victoria asked. The old road was bumpy and she thought perhaps Becki was being careful so as not to damage her vehicle. It was understandable, but Victoria didn't care about any vehicle. She knew Orpine was bad off by now. Every second counted. Besides, this vehicle was built for rugged terrain.

"Chill, would you. I'm going as fast as I can," Becki said.

Victoria glanced at Becki. There was something that troubled her. *Sure, she'd helped get the Trioxin, but how did she do it so easily*, Victoria wondered. *Why had it been so hard for her to get it, yet Becki had just walked into the medical facility and got some?*

Victoria took the bottle out of her pocket and examined it. She thought, *why am I so suspicious. I have Orpine's Trioxin. That's all that matters. Who cares how she got it?*

Becki glanced over at her. "What's the matter? Don't you believe it's the real thing?" She smiled.

Victoria blinked at the suggestion. She'd never doubted it was the real thing. Why should she?

"I just can't believe you were able to get it. It was so hard for me with no S.I.N. How'd you do it?"

"I told you, I got connections. Besides, I'm legal, you know?" Becki held up her hand. "I got my S.I.N. Makes all the difference."

Victoria frowned. "Yes. Connections." She looked at the bottle and opened it, pouring out several pills into the palm of her hand. They were blue, just like Orpine's Trioxin.

"Told ya." Becki quipped.

"What?" Victoria asked.

"They're real."

"Oh. I never doubted that. I just hope we get there in time to use them."

"How much further?"

"Not too much. About an hour and then we turn off for a little way before we hike the rest of the way."

"Hike?" Marelle asked from the back seat. "How far?"

"Five of six miles."

Victoria could tell Marelle was worried about her children. "You can stay in the car if you want and I'll come back for you in the morning."

"That's okay. We'll be all right."

Becki glanced at Victoria. "Mel said you have lots of currency at your cabin. He said that's why he was helping you."

Victoria wondered when Becki had discussed this with Mel. She nodded.

"How much?"

"We sold everything seven years ago."

"That doesn't tell me much. A ballpark figure?"

"How much do you want?" Victoria asked, figuring this had been Becki's objective all along.

"I don't want any."

"Isn't that why you're helping me? There must be a reason." Victoria detected a frown on Becki's face.

"I guess I'm offended, Victoria. I thought you liked me. I like you. Can't friends help friends?"

"Yes. Friends can and friends do, but you don't even know me. You saw me for the first time in the park yesterday. I'd say that makes us acquaintances at best. Hopefully to become friends, but that takes time."

Marelle spoke up from the back seat. "We are all linked by our common goals," she said, sounding like a communer again for a moment. "It's the universal connection. We're all linked by a great creative force so we help each other even if we don't know everyone. Lots of people do. Becki must be tuned in."

"I wish you'd said something sooner if you don't trust me," Becki said.

"I didn't say I don't trust you. Listen, I don't know what I'm saying. I'm just so worried about Orpine, and confused by what's happened since we left society seven years ago. I'm sorry, Becki. I really do appreciate your help. Really."

They rode in an uneasy silence for a while until Victoria pointed to the turn off. Soon, they parked the car and everyone got out.

"I should go the rest of the way alone," Victoria said.

"Are you crazy? I didn't come all this way to stop here," Becki said.

"I can run ahead and get there quicker by myself," Victoria said.

"Yeah, and if you get hurt, how quickly will you get there then? I don't want to get stuck out here and there's no way we could find you. We'd get lost for sure. No. I say we all stay together."

Victoria reluctantly agreed. "We have to hurry. I still think Marelle should wait here with the children."

"No way!" Jeremy said. "I want to come, too," Robin said. Marelle looked at her children and then at Victoria.

"They're used to hiking in the woods. Becki's right, we better stay together. I'd be lost out here by myself."

Victoria winked at Jeremy. "Well, let's go. We should be able to make it before dark."

Chapter 11

Your own worst enemy.

Victoria led the way, followed by Jeremy, Marelle and Robin, with Becki behind. Victoria wanted to go faster but slowed her pace for the sake of Marelle who lagged behind even though the children seemed to have no trouble keeping up.

A mile and a half into the woods, Victoria looked back to make sure everyone was coming along. Marelle and the children came up behind her. "Where's Becki?"

Marelle turned and looked back. "She was there a little while ago. I didn't notice her stop."

Victoria yelled, "Becki? Where are you?"

Becki came jogging up from the path. "Sorry, I had to make a rest stop," she said, panting.

"You should have said something. We'd have waited for you. You could have gotten lost," Victoria said.

"Not on this path. I can easily track you guys," Becki said as she caught her breath. "Come on, let's go. I hope you have food at your cabin, Victoria. I'm getting hungry." She pushed past Marelle and the children.

Victoria resumed the lead but her thoughts were not about food. The closer they got to the cabin, the more anxious Victoria became. She forgot about Becki and the others when she pushed through the thicket into the opening where the cottage stood. She caught her breath, smiled, and wiped a tear away at the same time.

It was quiet. Too quiet. She ran ahead, panicked by the silence. Where is Delight? Why isn't she barking?

She pushed the door open and ran inside the cabin. No one was there. She checked everywhere, even under the bed, calling Orpine. The food and water were still on the table next to his bed, untouched. Then she spotted the note on the counter.

She picked it up. It was folded into thirds with her name written in block letters on the outside, squiggly, as if by someone whose hands were shaking. It was Orpine's penmanship. She opened it just as the others came inside.

"Where's your husband?" Marelle asked, looking around.

The children jumped into the large chairs and relaxed, happy to have arrived at their destination.

Robin spotted the rag doll near the picture of Colleen and immediately grabbed it and hugged it to herself.

"What is it?" Becki asked.

"It's a note from Orpine." Victoria bit her lips.

"What does it say?" Marelle asked.

Victoria read it aloud, softly:

My dearest Victoria,

I can't let you return to find me dead.

Victoria paused and looked sadly at Marelle and Becki. She continued to read the note:

And I'm sure I will be dead before you get back--if you get back. I'm sorry I let you go. I'm sorry I made you come here in the first place. I'm sorry about everything. Please go back and make things right for yourself. Don't blame yourself. I know you tried to help me. It's not your fault.

Remember, I always loved you. Don't try to find me. I'm going to disappear and spend forever in the wilderness I love. When you hear the breeze whispering in the pine trees, you will hear me telling you I love you.

Your love forever, Orpine

Victoria sat down at the table, shaking.

Marelle put her arms around her. "I'm so sorry, Victoria," she said.

"I should have stayed here with him. I never should have left him to die alone."

"You did the right thing. Anyone would have done the same. You tried your best to save him," Marelle said.

"I'm too late. I'm always too late," Victoria cried bitterly.

"What's that noise?" Jeremy asked, looking out the window.

"What?" Robin asked, looking too.

"I hear something. It sounds like a plane," he said. Marelle noticed, too, and went over to the window to investigate.

"So, where do you keep the money?" Becki asked, sitting down opposite Victoria.

"What?"

"The currency? You said you keep it here. I'd like to see it. Where is it?"

Victoria looked deeply into Becki's eyes. "I have met you before yesterday, haven't I? I just can't place where."

"Where is the money?" Becki demanded.

Victoria pointed at the cabinet on the opposite side of the room. "Take all you want. I don't need it anymore."

Becki went to the cabinet and opened the door. She took out a large box and lifted off the lid. It was nearly full of money. Before she turned around, Victoria pushed her into the wall with as much force as she could muster. Becki fell headlong, stunned.

"What are you doing?" Marelle cried, turning from the window, shocked by Victoria's actions.

She instinctively reached for her children, pulling them close.

"Come on! Bring the kids! We gotta get out of here quick!" Victoria said as she bolted out the door.

Jeremy ran after her. "Come on Mom!"

Marelle followed, holding Robin's hand. Robin held onto the rag doll and it flopped after them. They ran for the woods just as a large dark helicopter circled over the cabin.

Becki ran outside looking for them.

"What's happening?" Marelle asked when she caught up to Victoria and Jeremy behind a large pine tree.

"I'm not sure but something is wrong. Look. Becki isn't the least bit concerned about that helicopter. It's almost like she was expecting it. See, she's signaling to them."

They watched from their hiding place as Becki waved to the copter pilot. They could barely hear her yelling over the noise of the helicopter.

"Everything is okay," she yelled. "I'm in control! I'm in complete control of the situation!"

"Oh my God," Victoria whispered. "I've heard that voice before. She's the B.C.T. agent from the store."

They watched in disbelief as Becki pulled off the blonde wig and her own dark hair fell free.

"B.C.T.?" Marelle asked, searching Victoria's face.

"Remember, when I was stopped that first day at the convenience store. She's the agent that tried to arrest me. I knew it was too easy. I think she let me escape. She's must have been following me ever since."

"Why?" Marelle asked desperately.

"Maybe she thought I'd lead the authorities to dissidents," Victoria said.

Victoria saw Marelle was frightened for herself and her children. "Maybe we should just give ourselves up and explain to them what's happened," Victoria suggested.

"Are you crazy? Do you know what they do to non-conformers? They'll take my children away and I'll never see them again. We'll both go to jail for a long time. If it's the B.C.T. that's after us, we've got to get out of here!" Marelle cried.

"Becki has too much evidence on us now. They'll never believe us. You don't understand how determined these people are when they think you're a non-conformer. They hate non-conformers!"

"Let's go back to the Land Rover," Victoria said.

"No," Marelle said, looking up.

"No, the helicopters will see that. There must be someplace we can hide?"

Victoria thought for a moment. "Follow me. I think I know a place."

She led them to the stream, wading down and then across. Marelle carried Robin who cried at the cold water. They headed towards the hills rather than back toward the cabin. Further downstream, they ran up an embankment and into the thick Maine woods.

Victoria led the way as fast as she could while keeping an eye on Marelle and the children. Jeremy caught up to her and pulled her arm.

"Stop. My Mom can't keep running," he said.

Victoria saw that Marelle was falling behind and realized something was wrong. She went back. "Are you okay?"

"Can you carry Robin?" Marelle asked.

"Sure," Victoria said. "Come with me, Robin."

The child clung to her mother.

"It's okay, sweetie. Go with Victoria."

Victoria took Robin into her arms. The little girl clung exceptionally tightly.

Marelle slowly lowered herself to the ground.

Victoria knelt down and looked into her eyes. "What is it?"

Marelle's lips trembled and she moaned in pain. "I can't keep going." Tears fell down her face. She looked at the ground sadly.

"What is it?" Victoria repeated desperately, looking around.

"I'm bleeding," Marelle whispered, looking back at Victoria. "I'm pregnant."

Victoria gasped. "God, Marelle. Why didn't you say something?"

Marelle groaned again. "I can't go on. Take Robin and Jeremy and get away."

"I'm not leaving," Robin cried.

Jeremy stood above his mother and looked at Victoria desperately. "I'm not leaving my mother either," he said.

Victoria put Robin down and knelt closer to Marelle. "We're staying together. I'm not leaving you."

A helicopter swooped over the treetops not far from their location. "Let me help you," Victoria said, putting her arm around Marelle.

"Jeremy, you bring your sister. Let's hurry!"

"I can't go on," Marelle cried.

"Come on, Mom. I'll help you," Jeremy said.

"I can't make it. Take the children, Victoria. The police have heat sensors and will soon locate us. You must find a place to hide with my children."

Victoria pulled Marelle to her feet. "Come on, it's not far. You can make it."

Robin clung to Victoria's leg. She was surprised how tightly the little girl held on.

Jeremy grabbed his sister and they hobbled forward. "Mom's going to be okay," he said to Robin. "You're going to be okay, too."

They stopped in the woods when the terrain began to climb steeply.

"I can't go any further," Marelle said, obviously growing weaker.

"We've got to get medical help for you," Victoria said, kneeling by her side. Robin clung and looked away as if not wanting to see her mother suffer.

"I know a place not far from here where we'll be safe. You can make it. Let me help you."

Victoria pushed Robin towards her brother and helped Marelle. Jeremy ignored Robin's cries and took the other side of his mother.

"This way. Hurry." Victoria said.

They headed up the incline towards the rocky terrain until they came to a hidden cave. They stopped outside of it and Marelle lay down to rest on the ground.

"It looks dark in there," Robin said.

"I'll go inside first," Victoria said, "just to make sure we don't disturb anything."

"Cool," Jeremy said.

"I don't like this place," Robin whined.

"Do bears live in there?" Jeremy said.

Victoria smiled. "Sometimes, but usually not in the summer." She glanced around. The sun was setting. It would soon be dark. "Wait here."

She crawled inside. It was dark and cool. She felt the floor and sides and then heard some squeaking noises above her. "Oh, shit!" she cried, lying close to the ground. "Watch out!"

Suddenly, dozens of bats flew out of the cavern. She heard the children screech and scooted back outside.

"It's okay. You can go inside now."

"There's bats in there," Robin pouted.

"They're all gone now," Victoria said.

Jeremy took his sister's hand and dragged her inside with him. "Come on. You can't be a baby now."

Victoria helped Marelle inside and laid her down against the cave wall. "Is Mommy okay?" Robin asked, nudging closer to Victoria.

"She needs to rest," Victoria said. She removed her own jacket and placed it over Marelle who was shivering uncontrollably. Jeremy sat close to Victoria. Robin stayed close on the other side. Time passed and it grew dark.

Frightened, worried about their mother, and overcome by the flight, the children finally dozed.

Marelle stirred in the early morning light and sat up. Victoria smiled at her. "Feeling better?"

Marelle shrugged. "A little."

Victoria looked at her for a long moment, not wanting to pry.

"Danny is the father," Marelle whispered.

Victoria nodded.

Marelle bit her lip sadly. "He said being a father wasn't in his reality."

"I'm sorry, Marelle. He seemed like the perfect father when he was with Jeremy and Robin."

"Master has other plans for him. He's grooming him to be a big shot leader in the group. I guess having children would have been too much of a distraction."

"That's too bad," Victoria said.

"He was right," Marelle said. "Danny was right."

"He was right about what?" Victoria asked.

"Having a baby wasn't in his reality. Not anymore." Victoria's eyes widened with realization.

Marelle nodded. "I've lost the baby." She wiped a tear from her eyes.

Victoria moved closer and put her arms around Marelle who sobbed uncontrollably for several minutes. Tears rolled down Victoria's face, too.

A couple hours later the children stirred. Victoria heard a noise in the distance and crawled to the opening of the cave. She squinted in the bright morning sunlight and strained to hear.

Barking! A dog was approaching.

"Come on. We have to get moving. Someone is coming!"

Marelle sat up. "Are you going to be able to keep going?" Victoria asked.

She nodded. "I think I can make it, now. I actually feel much better."

"I'm hungry," Robin complained.

"We'll find some food later when we're safe. Right now, we have to move on. A dog will sniff us out and we'll be trapped if we stay in here. Besides, the bats have come back."

Robin and Jeremy looked up and gasped. They ran outside and waited for Victoria and their mother. Then they all hurried back into the woods.

"Where are we going?" Jeremy asked.

Victoria didn't know, but she couldn't tell him that. "First things first," she said. "We have to get away from the authorities and then we'll find the others and figure out what to do from there."

"What others?" Jeremy asked.

"I can't run so fast," Robin cried. "My side hurts." Robin held tight to Marelle's hand.

"I can't carry you, Robin. Let Victoria help you."

"Here. I can carry you," Victoria said, picking up the child.

"What others?" Jeremy repeated.

"Huh? Oh, the others my husband associated with. Ralph and his friends. They'll know what to do."

"How far away are they?" Jeremy asked.

Victoria gulped. It had taken a day by vehicle to get to them. She looked at Jeremy. "Don't worry. We'll get there."

The barking dog got closer as Victoria and the children reached a thick spruce grove. Large boulders pushed through the ground from years of frost heaves, and large spruce tree roots knotted and gnarled around them. She found a good hiding spot and put Robin down, surprised at how heavy she was to carry. She leaned back against the rock to catch her breath and glanced at Marelle. "How are you doing?" she asked.

Marelle smiled weakly and nodded. "I'll be okay." The dog's bark sounded familiar to Victoria. She looked around the corner.

"Delight!" she cried, recognizing the approaching dog. "Here, girl. We're over here."

The dog sniffed and approached apprehensively at first, then recognized Victoria. Delight whined loudly and rolled around happily for several minutes, crying in excitement. "It's okay, girl. Shhhh...quiet down...come on...yes, I'm happy to see you, too." She hugged the dog lovingly.

"You're dog sure is emotional," Jeremy observed.

"She's still a puppy. And she's been alone for several days. She'll calm down in a few minutes."

Victoria stroked the dog's ears. "You know where Orpine went, don't you, girl? If only you could talk. You were with him." She hugged the dog again, wiping tears from her face. "I'm glad you were with him. We'll come back when this is over and find his body for a proper burial."

Jeremy watched over the rock. "Look!" he hollered.

213

"What is it?"

"The helicopter is back."

Delight licked Victoria's hands when she stopped patting her. "Do you think they saw the dog?" she asked, looking out.

"I don't know, but they probably will be coming soon" Jeremy observed.

"You're right about that. They can track anyone who has a S.I.N. implant" She looked at Marelle, remembering Henry's comments about finding lost children.

Marelle felt her right hand. "Too bad we can't remove it."

Victoria pulled out her gray plastic knife. Marelle nodded approval at the unspoken suggestion.

"Do me first," she said, holding out her hand.

"Where is it?" Victoria asked.

Marelle felt around for a minute. "Here, you can barely feel it. It's the size of a grain of rice, just below the skin. Let me see your knife."

Marelle couldn't cut out her own S.I.N. because she wasn't dexterous enough with her left hand.

"You'll have to do it," she said, handing the knife back to Victoria.

Victoria took the knife. She held Marelle's hand securely and glanced at the two children who were watching silently. She made a tiny slit and a drop of blood formed on Marelle's hand.

Marelle wiped it away and nodded for Victoria to continue. She pried the implant out like a giant splinter. It was shaped like a tiny pellet. She placed it on a nearby rock.

"Did it hurt, Mommy? Robin asked.

"Not much, honey. Let me see your hand."

While Marelle carefully removed her children's implants, Victoria watched for any sign of pursuers. The three little pellets were on the rock, barely visible.

"What do we do with them?" Marelle asked.

Victoria picked up a smooth rock and raised her hand and smashed them.

"Come on. We have to move quickly. And keep out of sight. Stay close to me."

They headed further into the forest with Delight running back and forth on their trail. Victoria remembered Orpine's admonition about the dog giving her away. She wouldn't care if it were just her, but now she had Marelle and her two children to consider. She knew what she might have to do if the situation arose. She clasped the gray knife inside her pocket and glanced back at the dog.

Victoria glanced over her shoulder frequently. There was a thick growth of new forest just a little further. It had been cut off for lumber a year before they moved to the cabin and was now a haven for wildlife. It was a great place to hide. They could get lost in the thick growth if they could just get there in time. Orpine and she had hunted there on many occasions. She wished he was with her now.

When they stopped to catch their breath, Victoria found a fruit bar in her pocket. Becki had given it to her the day before. She handed it to Marelle.

Marelle broke it in two and gave it all to the children. "You need to eat some, too," Victoria said.

"I'm okay," Marelle said, but both Jeremy and Robin broke their part in half. Jeremy handed his half to Victoria and Robin handed hers to her mother.

"You raised them well," Victoria said.

Soon, they ran on. Victoria watched the trail behind them, listening for any sign of being followed. Delight ran alongside her, panting. "You want some water, don't you girl?" she said, realizing suddenly how thirsty she was herself. "Soon."

Robin began to tire.

"Let's go," Victoria said, picking her up again.

They hurried further, as the helicopter hovered over the treetops behind them near where they'd spent the night. Victoria suspected they had found the cave by now.

They came to the new growth section in about an hour. The going became immediately difficult with briars and branches pulling and smacking at them.

She held Robin close protectively. Jeremy followed behind with Marelle and Delight.

"Try not to break any branches. They'll go back real quick because they're so pliable and no one will find our path," she said.

"Who'd want to?" Jeremy said. "This place is a jungle."

"That's the whole idea. Come on. Hurry."

Twenty minutes later, Victoria heard the helicopter land somewhere behind them. She could faintly hear voices hollering over the noise of the copter's blades. Then it lifted off. She knew they were getting close. So did Jeremy.

Delight barked. "Shhh..." Victoria scolded, glancing at the dog.

"Are you sure you know what you're doing?" Jeremy asked.

"You got a better idea?"

"No." The going was slow and tedious. The pursuers were closing in. Delight grew agitated and barked. Victoria felt the gray plastic knife in her pocket along with the prescription bottle.

"Come on. We gotta hurry! They are gaining on us," Victoria cried.

They ran to the other side of the thick undergrowth and came to an old shack near a small lake.

"Can you guys swim?"

"Like fish," Marelle said.

"Come on." They went into the water, gasping from the shock of the cold. The pond was spring fed from the mountain run-off, so it never warmed much, not even in the summer.

Delight drank for a minute before jumping in after them. They swam to a small island near the middle of the pond. Delight shook when she got to the island and barked, waiting for them to catch up to her. "Shhh..."Victoria scolded futilely. The dog ran back and forth, barking.

"Marelle, take your children into the trees and hide. I'll catch up to you in a minute."

"What are you going to do?"

"Never mind. JUST GO!"

Victoria held the shivering dog close for a quick moment. She could hear voices back on the shore and knew they would be coming through the woods any minute.

"I'm real sorry, girl. You know I love you." She wiped her face with her wet sleeve and sniffed.

"Orpine was right. You're going to give us away."

The dog licked her face, whining. Victoria put her hand over Delight's eyes and picked up a rock. "I'm so sorry, girl."

Chapter 12

Escape from Paradise

Saturday July 2nd, 2026

Victoria caught up to Marelle and the children. "Where's Delight?" Jeremy asked immediately, but she didn't answer. He looked at her suspiciously.

Victoria pointed back towards the shore where they had come. "They're going to come through over there," she said. "We're going to swim back over to the other side. It'll take them a while to find our trail, maybe enough time for us to get away."

"The water is awfully cold," Robin complained, still shivering. She clung to her mother.

"I know it is, but you'll dry off on the other side. You're a good swimmer."

"We had lessons," Robin said.

"Why isn't your dog coming?" Jeremy asked.

Marelle surmised what Victoria had done. "We better hurry," she said.

Victoria gave Marelle a grateful look. "Let's go, kids. Ready?"

Back into the water they went and swam to the other side. It didn't seem as cold as the first time. Victoria kept a watchful eye on the other shoreline. They scooted behind some fallen logs just as the B.C.T. agents came out of the woods on the opposite shore.

Following the tracks, the agents pointed across the water to the small island.

We've bought ourselves some time, Victoria thought.

But we better hurry!

"Come on," she whispered. "Let's get out of here." For two hours they made their way through the woods. Victoria kept a watchful eye on Marelle to make sure she was okay. When they stopped to rest, Robin started crying.

"It's okay, dear," Marelle comforted. They all sat down on a large fallen log.

"I lost my dolly," Robin cried.

"That's the second dolly you've lost," Jeremy teased.

"Where did you drop her?" Victoria asked, hating to part with yet another memory of Colleen.

"I donno," Robbin said, shrugging.

"That wasn't your doll," Jeremy quipped.

"It's all alright, Jeremy. She can have the doll. I'm just worried that they'll find it and know which way we went."

"She had it in the cave last night," Jeremy said, hoping to be helpful.

Robin looked at Victoria and sniffed.

"It's okay, dear. We can find you another doll," Marelle said.

Victoria looked back and couldn't hear anyone following. "We better keep going. You guys are doing great," she said. Marelle nodded.

They headed on. Periodically, Victoria stopped to check the direction of the sun. They were heading northwest. Victoria was confident she could survive in the wilderness by herself, but worried about Marelle and the children. They didn't have any supplies or extra clothing, and Marelle still needed medical attention.

"I'm hungry," Robin said.

Victoria looked around. Up ahead there was a small clearing. She spied some purple burdocks.

"Wait here," she said, taking the gray knife out of her pocket. She cut some stems and peeled them. After snipping off the shoots, she handed it to Robin. Then she did the same for Jeremy and Marelle. And then for herself.

"Eat. It's good," she said, grinning at their expressions. She took a bite of hers to show them.

Jeremy bit first. He mulled it over in his mouth, then ate it. Soon they had each eaten the whole thing. Victoria cut more and gave the knife to Jeremy so he could harvest some, too. It was moist, sweet, and refreshing.

"Watch out for the prickers," she called after him. "And don't lose the knife."

She showed them more edible plants and after an hour they were satisfied. "We need to keep going to get as far as we can today," she said after they were rejuvenated.

Feeling more confident, Victoria slowed the pace in the afternoon. An hour later Jeremy stopped behind her.

"What is it?" she asked.

"I hear someone following us," he said, glaring at Robin. "They probably found the doll you dropped?"

"No they didn't," Robin glared back.

"Shhh...." Marelle chastised.

Victoria went behind the children. "Go on, you keep going up ahead," she said. She listened for a moment. Jeremy was correct-someone or something was following them. She could hear the crack of twigs and the crunch of dry leaves behind them.

"Could be an animal," she said.

Robin looked back, eyes wide. "What kind of animal?"

"Maybe a bear or a wolf or a mountain lion," Jeremy said.

"Or maybe a person," Marelle said, taking Robin's hand and hurrying them along.

Marelle was right. It was obvious the person was getting closer. They ran as fast as they could, becoming disoriented in the woods and finally going in a large circle.

"Stop right there!" a voice bellowed.

"It was Becki. Victoria turned around. Becki held a weapon pointed right at her. Marelle pulled the children behind her protectively. Both peeked around to see Becki.

"Becki, let us go. We aren't any threat to your system," Victoria pleaded.

Becki raised her weapon higher. Victoria remembered Orpine's war games and thought, this definitely feels real. He had instructed her to shoot first without hesitation. But he hadn't told her what to do if she didn't have any weapon.

"You really don't get it, do you?" Becki said.

"I know one thing, Becki. My husband and I just wanted to live alone, by ourselves. We weren't a threat to anyone and we didn't hurt anyone. Now he's dead."

"It's his own fault," Becki said unsympathetically.

"No. You're wrong. It's not his fault," Victoria cried.

"He served his country. He paid his own way. He didn't deserve to die like this. My daughter didn't deserve to die! It's not his fault; it's not her fault; it's not my fault!"

Becki motioned to her to raise her hands. She pulled restraints from her back pocket. She pressed a button on her wristband and spoke into it. "Follow my signal. I got them."

Victoria looked around for a possible escape route.

"You were using me," Victoria said realizing that Becki must have been communicating with the authorities all along the way when she disappeared before on the trail to the cabin and back at the store when she was gone so long. "You trapped me."

"Just doing my job."

"You job? Tracking down women and children?"

"My job is stopping the dissidents. We know what they're planning to do."

"What they're planning to do?"

"We know all about it," Becki glared.

"You sound just like they do. They believe you're going to attack them, and you believe they're going to attack you," Victoria said.

"Subversives only have one goal: to overthrow the government."

"I know these people. They aren't planning to do anything except to protect themselves."

"We know they're planning to attack soon," Becki said.

"That's absurd. No one is planning to overthrow the government. My God, do you really think they'd be that crazy?"

"We know they are just that extreme. That's why they're so dangerous. Maybe you aren't deeply involved enough to be aware of that, but our surveillance shows the militia's conducting war practices. Their own literature talks about going to war with the government. It's been coming for a long time. We know that."

"You're wrong," Victoria said. "You're dead wrong!"

"If we are, then the courts will decide. My job is to bring you in and that's what I'm going to do at any cost."

"Do you have any idea what it cost Marelle?"

"Don't," Marelle said to Victoria. "I don't want her to have the satisfaction."

"That's too bad. It's her own fault for getting mixed up with you Cling-On's in the first place."

"Too bad? That's all you can say? She lost her baby for God's sake! Why? Because of some currency system? Becki, that doesn't make any sense. Advanced technology doesn't mean it's always used for good. People have a right to question changes."

"Non-conformers have to be stopped."

"You're talking about regular people who don't want the government controlling all their affairs-people who people believe the Constitution."

"Non-conformers are going to ruin the whole system. Don't you understand, Victoria? Everyone has to be on the network for it to work. Everyone. No more cheaters spoiling it for the law-abiding citizens. Believe whatever you want but conform to the legally instituted system."

"It's not fair," Victoria said.

"It's not fair for some to conform and others not to," Becki said. "I know your kind. So sanctimonious. Quoting the Constitution like a Bible-Thumper. All the time, cheating the system. Not paying taxes. Not supporting the services provided by the government. Others end up paying your share. That's what's not fair!"

"We haven't cheated anyone," Marelle said, clutching her children fearfully.

Becki's demeanor had changed. There was a hatefulness about her.

"The courts will decide that. It's my job to bring the whole lot of you in and that's what I'm going to do."

"But look at what you're doing," Victoria pleaded. "You're making things worse. You said you wanted to be my friend. You told me I could trust you." She could hear the desperation in her own voice. A helicopter roared in the distance and was getting closer.

"DROP YOUR GUN!" A man called from behind Becki. Victoria recognized the voice.

"NOW!" the man yelled, shooting into a tree to Becki's left.

Slowly, Becki lowered her weapon to the ground, all the while glaring at Victoria. "I would never be friends with the likes of you," she snarled.

"Put it on the ground and step away," the man commanded.

Becki glared at Victoria and Marelle. "You're not going to escape. You're just making it worse for yourself and those children."

Marelle pulled her children closer.

Mel walked out of the woods keeping his weapon aimed at Becki. Victoria couldn't believe it. Jeremy ran over to him. "Who are you?" he asked happily.

"Get her restraints," he told Victoria.

Mel secured Becki's hands behind her. Then he took her wristband and placed it on a rock and smashed it with the butt of his rifle. "That ought to stop them for a little while."

"Cool," Jeremy said.

Mel went over to Robin and handed her the Rag Doll. "Did you lose this?"

She nodded and hugged the doll. "You found her!"

Victoria smiled, then looked at Mel quizzically. He ignored her unspoken question. He didn't know why he was here. Maybe it was something she said back at the farm. Maybe he just got tired of being a jerk.

"I found the doll in the woods and figured I better pick it up so no one else would find it," he said. "I've been following you since you left the farm."

He turned to Becki and pulled her arm. "Come on," he said gruffly.

"Where are we going?" Becki demanded.

"You'll find out soon enough."

They hurried after Mel who led them in the opposite direction of the approaching helicopter. A few miles into the dense woods, he secured Becki to a tree with her hands bound behind her. The woods were thick and dark.

"You can't leave me here," Becki called as they walked away.

"Don't worry. Your friends will find you eventually, but we'll be long gone by then." Mel turned to Victoria. "Come on. Let's make tracks. They'll stop searching after dark. She'll be found in the morning at the latest."

"Is she going to be all right?" Victoria asked.

"Better than we would have been if she got her way," he said.

"But I feel bad leaving her like that," Victoria said.

"It's the right thing to do," Mel said. "Don't worry. She's got her S.I.N. They'll find her." He headed out.

With one last glance back at Becki, Victoria turned and caught up to Mel, Marelle and the children. His compass made finding their way easier and without further stops, they hiked through much of the night.

Victoria carried Robin and Mel carried Jeremy when the children grew tired. The sun was just peeking over the horizon when they smelled a familiar aroma. Coffee.

They rounded a hill to see a camper in a small clearing. It was a tent hauled on a trailer behind an all-terrain vehicle. Victoria recognized the large burly man pouring a cup of coffee. It was Ralph.

She ran over to him. Marelle, Mel and the children stood back.

Ralph looked up startled. "Victoria!"

"I can't believe it," she cried, happy to see their old friend. She wrapped her arms around him and hugged him for a long moment, holding back her tears.

Marelle realized Victoria knew the man so she hurried over to them.

"We found you just in time," Marelle said breathlessly. "I couldn't go on much further and neither could the children."

"Children?" Ralph said.

"What are you doing way out here?" Victoria asked.

Ralph frowned. "I told you folks I was going to do some fishing up your way, remember. Besides, I needed to get away and do some thinking. Judy wants to go back and find Coralee."

"Coralee?" Victoria said.

Ralph studied her. "You know where Coralee is?"

"Yes. Ralph. I don't think she wants to be found. Not now."

"Is she safe?"

"Yes. She's fine. She's at a farm on the other side of Woodinville."

"Not one of those communers?"

Victoria smiled. "No. I don't think Coralee will ever be a communer. I think she just wants a normal life. Give her some time."

"Normal life. Whatever the hell that is," Ralph sniffed.

"Did you catch any fish?" Victoria asked.

"Nope. Didn't expect to find what I did, though," he said somberly.

Victoria felt a pain in the pit of her stomach. "What is it, Ralph?"

"Come with me," he said, turning towards the camper. Victoria noticed a second coffee cup on the fireplace. He opened the tent flap and held it for Victoria to enter.

"Orpine!" she exclaimed. He was lying on a cot in the corner.

"He's bad off, Victoria," Ralph said, shaking his head sadly. "Keeps calling your name."

"How'd he get here?" she asked as she climbed inside.

"I found him wandering out in the woods. That dog of yours was barking to beat the band. I never would have found Orpine if it wasn't for that dog."

Victoria's eyes watered and she looked away at the thought of Delight.

"Ayah, that dog of yours weren't about to leave her sick master's side. Until the other night. She just took off. I couldn't imagine where she went. She must 'a knew you needed her, too. Some dog."

Victoria reached for Orpine's forehead. He was weak, but opened his eyes and smiled at her. "Victoria," he whispered.

"Don't talk," she said. "I'm here. I told you I'd come back." She pulled the prescription bottle from her pocket. "I got the Trioxin. She quickly took out some of the little blue pills and put them in Orpine's mouth.

"Water," she said to Ralph.

"Be right back," he said, hurrying to get it.

Orpine swallowed a tiny amount of water and the pills, and fell immediately back to sleep.

"Do you think I'm too late?" Victoria asked.

"It's supposed to work fast," Ralph offered. "When he wakes up, give him another one. A double dose. Maybe it'll help. Nothing to lose at this stage."

Victoria looked at Orpine sadly. Ralph patted her shoulder. "You can't do anymore now. Come outside and have something to eat. You need to keep up your strength."

"Thank you, Ralph," Victoria said.

"I didn't do anything," he said.

"Thank you for finding Orpine. I was so afraid," she said, biting her lip.

"Don't think about that now," Ralph whispered.

"I was so afraid he'd died out there all alone," she whispered.

"Come outside. I'll get you some coffee."

They went back outside. Mel and Marelle stood over by the fire as the children played nearby.

"Ralph, I'd like to introduce Mel," Victoria said. "He rescued us when the B.C.T. had us cornered." She smiled at Mel. "He's a Vet, too."

"Glad to meet you, Mel. Thank you for helping Victoria. She's a special person."

Victoria blushed. "This is Marelle and those are her children, Jeremy and Robin."

"You look a mite pale, Miss," Ralph observed.

Victoria noticed, too. She'd been so worried about Orpine that she hadn't realized how much Marelle was suffering with the loss of her pregnancy, but she knew it was a private secret and didn't share it with Ralph and Mel.

"Help yourself to coffee," Ralph said, pulling out some more cups. "I got some food here, too. Bet you kids are hungry, aren't you?"

They both nodded. Ralph cooked eggs and potatoes for breakfast. Victoria kept checking Orpine, but he remained sleeping.

An hour later, after cleaning up the campsite and putting out the fire, Ralph announced they should be moving on.

"I agree," Mel said. "It's only a matter of time until they catch up to us, once they figure out which direction we went."

"We took out our S.I.N.'s," Robin said, holding her hand up to Mel.

"So you did."

Jeremy held up his hand, too. "See, right there."

"Smart." Mel said.

Victoria rode in the back, sitting beside Orpine. Marelle and the children rode inside the camper with them. Mel rode alongside Ralph.

When they stopped two hours later, Victoria got out. "He's getting worse," she told Ralph. "His fever is high and he's shaking. I don't know what to do."

Mel climbed down from the vehicle and looked inside the camper. "Let me see that Trioxin."

"What?" Victoria said, surprised.

"Let me see your prescription."

He spotted the bottle and grabbed it.

"You can't have them," she said, "not while Orpine is still alive!"

"I don't want them," Mel said.

"Is that why you followed us?" Victoria suddenly distrusted Mel, despite all her instincts not to. She couldn't stop herself. "You wanted the money all along, didn't you?"

He looked at her briefly, then opened the container. "They must be worth a lot on the black market. That's what you want, isn't it?" Victoria spit the words at him, confused and upset with Orpine's deteriorating condition.

Mel tasted on of the pills. "Here's your problem," he said.

"What are you talking about?"

"Sugar."

Victoria looked stunned. "What?

"Sugar. These are nothing but sugar. This isn't Trioxin. Trioxin has a bitter taste. See for yourself."

She grabbed the container, spilling the pills everywhere. She put one in her mouth. It was sugar!

"I take Trioxin, remember? This isn't the real thing. One tablet of Trioxin might have helped him. They never intended for him to live," Mel said.

"I don't understand. Why? Why would Becki do this?" Victoria cried, looking from Ralph to Mel.

"They don't want any non-conformers," Ralph stated. "We are a threat to their system. It's power, Victoria. Plain and Simple. That's why they burned down my store. They know we can't survive out here without supplies. They know the Vets will die without Trioxin. It's all about power, their power. We are the enemy and they want to destroy us."

"Anyone who doesn't have a S.I.N. is a threat. We don't have any rights. That's why Becki tricked you. She wasn't about to give you Trioxin, not when they deliberately cut off your husbands supply," Mel said.

"We must be eliminated because we threaten their control," Ralph said.

Victoria looked at Mel. "I'm sorry I said those things," she said.

Mel shifted his weight uneasily. "Forget it. I'd have thought the same thing in your shoes. How do you know who to trust anymore? How do any of us know who to believe?"

"They've killed Orpine. If he dies, it's their fault, as sure as if they'd shot him with a gun."

Mel reached into his backpack and pulled out a jar. "Here," he said to Victoria, "take this."

She looked at him.

"It's Trioxin. Give it to your husband."

She grabbed the jar. "Thank you, Mel." She hurried inside the camper. Orpine was barely conscious, but she got two tablets down his throat with a little water. He coughed and choked.

The trip was bumpy and rolly, but quicker than walking and by noon they approached the militia camp a few miles from Cappy and Edith's' cabin near the burned Wilderness Store.

When they came to a stop, Victoria and Marelle looked outside the camper. Ralph and Mel were already talking to the Commander. There were a dozen round earth houses well camouflaged under the canopy of tall trees. There was no sign of anyone else. Everyone must be inside, perhaps in hiding, Victoria surmised.

Victoria looked up at the bright sky. It was quiet and there were no helicopters. She wondered if Becki had been found yet, and if they were close behind. She climbed out of the camper and approached Ralph.

"We need to get Orpine inside," Ralph said, getting back on the All-Terrain Vehicle. She watched him drive around to one of the earth houses. Several men helped Ralph lift Orpine, cot and all, and carry him inside. She followed close behind.

Inside, there were several others lying on cots, too. They were all sick. She looked from the two women on one side of the room to the three men on the other, then to the nurse in the middle.

"R.I.T.S.?" Victoria asked.

The woman nodded. "Most of the Trioxin is gone. If we don't get more, they'll be dozens of sick Vets soon. Two have died already. There's nothing we can do."

Victoria looked at Mel who was standing quietly inside the door. He'd given Orpine the last of his prescription, too. Suddenly she realized the sacrifice of his act and felt even more remorse over her verbal attack. He walked out of the house. The nurse put a heavy quilt over Orpine and administered a shot. Orpine groaned lightly.

"He's not improving. I gave him extra Trioxin, but his condition is deteriorating," Victoria told the nurse.

She nodded sadly. "Probably too late," she said. "How long did he go without his Trioxin?"

Victoria thought for a moment, trying to remember exactly when he ran out. "I can't say for sure. I think he kept it from me," she said. "At least a week."

The nurse sighed deeply. "Two days will cause a relapse. Some of the Vets have tried to take half their dosage hoping it will last longer, but most of them start showing symptoms even then within a week."

Ralph and Victoria stayed by Orpine's bedside through the afternoon and evening. "I'm too late," Victoria lamented, holding his hands. He'd remained unconscious since they arrived.

Marelle put her arms around Victoria and sat with her for several hours while Ralph rested. Victoria had gotten the last pill down his throat in the middle of the night despite the nurses' protests. She'd said it would be better to give it to someone who was still healthy. Victoria knew she should have returned them to Mel. He hadn't asked. But she knew she should have.

"Who is that man?" Robin asked when she came inside looking for her mother early in the morning.

"That's Victoria's husband," Jeremy answered coming in behind her.

"You shouldn't come in here," Marelle said, sending the children back outside.

Edith came inside. "How's Orpine?" she asked.

"Not good," Victoria said without looking at her.

Edith frowned. "Too bad. He was a good soldier. You should be proud of him. He was the Lord's good soldier."

"He's not gone yet," Marelle said, defending her friend, immediately disliking Edith.

"Who are you? I don't remember seeing you around here?"

"This is Marelle. She's my friend," Victoria said.

"Those your kids?"

"Yes. We're not from around here," Marelle said.

Edith sized up her outfit and beads. "I guessed that."

"Don't pick on Marelle, Edith. She's had a hard time of it," Victoria said.

"No harder than the rest of us. We have to learn to carry the burdens the Lord gives us and not complain. We should be thankful."

Marelle bristled. "My view of the Lord is a bit different than yours!"

"That's too bad," Edith said.

"I don't know what you mean, too bad. I happen to be glad about that fact," Marelle said.

Victoria injected, "Look you two. You aren't that far apart you know."

Marelle and Edith stared at Victoria horrified. "You're not so different," Victoria persisted. "You, Edith. You want some concept of God to decide everything for yourself. You're a follower."

Before Edith could retort, Victoria addressed Marelle. "And you, Marelle. You've listened to disembodied spirits telling you who to marry and how to live. You two are not so different."

Orpine groaned and Victoria turned to him. Both women looked on silently, wanting to argue her statement, but holding back. Each was certain she was mistaken.

Victoria sniffed. Her tears were drying out and she wondered that she had any emotional strength left. Mel came inside.

"Got something," he said.

Victoria looked up. He held out another jar of Trioxin. "Where did you get that?" Victoria asked.

"I went to every Vet in the area and told them what happened. Many of them donated some of their own pills. There're about two dozen tablets in here. It'll help."

Victoria looked away sadly. "You keep them, Mel. You gave yours to Orpine, now you need it."

Mel stood silently.

Victoria stood up and took his hand. "Thank you, Mel. I'm sorry I called you a jerk. You're not a bad person. You've just had a hell of a lot of bad stuff happen to you."

He looked her in the eye and she saw the real man inside, not the druggie who'd rode with her to Woodinville.

She smiled. "Welcome back to the human race, Mel."

"It doesn't matter much," the nurse said. "Everyone will be out of Trioxin soon."

Orpine moaned and Victoria let go of Mel's hand and turned to her husband. "He's waking up," she said hopefully.

Ralph had returned and stood beside the cot. He glanced sadly at Mel and both men understood that Orpine was nearing the end. They'd seen death in the war. They recognized the symptoms.

"Orpine? Can you hear me?"

He opened his eyes and smiled faintly. "Victoria," he whispered, no longer shaking.

"Orpine. I'm here. I love you. Please don't leave me. I can't live without you," she choked, holding his hand.

"Don't cry," Orpine whispered. "I'm not in any pain."

She looked deeply into his eyes. No words seemed adequate, or necessary.

"I love you, Victoria."

She whispered. "I love you, too."

"You never truly die if you leave behind offspring. Remember what the Shaman told us."

Victoria thought he was delirious. "Gay Feathers?" she asked.

"Old Stormy Gay Feathers knew what he was talking about," Orpine said, smiling.

"He did?" she asked.

Orpine looked at her solemnly. "The old man's potion worked. He knew what he was doing."

Victoria realized suddenly that she was pregnant. Orpine must have sensed it, too. The cure was to provide offspring. She didn't know how she knew, but suddenly she was certain.

"Give our son love and freedom to run in the pine groves and frolic in the warm summer rain," Orpine whispered. He grieved knowing he would not be there to enjoy it.

"Orpine, I can't go on without you," Victoria sobbed.

"When the wind whispers in your ears, I'll be telling you how much I love you," Orpine said. "And when the raindrops tap you on the shoulder, I'll be giving you a little kiss," he smiled. "When the sun smiles on your face, I'll be smiling at you and our son. I'll never really leave you."

Victoria understood. Orpine knew all along he was going to die. She couldn't save him, just like she couldn't save Colleen. He was going to be free from pain and free from anguish she could barely comprehend. As sad as the moment was, there was also something else. He was at peace.

"Colleen is here now waiting for me," he whispered. Victoria was startled at this revelation, then happy.

"She says to tell you she loves you. We'll both be here for you when your time comes."

Victoria wiped her tears and sniffed. She felt overwhelmed. "I love you, Orpine."

He smiled weakly. "Have I told you lately that I love you?" he whispered.

She gently kissed his lips. Her eyes closed and when she opened them, she knew he was gone.

Ralph looked down and Mel left the house. "He's gone, Victoria," Ralph said. "Here, let me help you."

She sobbed uncontrollably for several minutes. Marelle came over to her and put her arms around her. "You did your best," she whispered.

Weakened by the ordeal and overcome with grief, Victoria collapsed.

Chapter 13

Never Easy to Say Good-Bye

When Victoria woke two hours later, Judy was sitting next to her bed. Ralph came inside and stood behind Judy. "Are you feeling any better?" he asked.

She remembered Orpine had died. "Where is everyone?" she asked.

"Getting ready to leave," Judy said.

"We're moving further into the wilderness," Ralph said. "The authorities will be looking for us. Some of the children and elderly have already left."

"Where's Orpine?" Victoria asked.

Judy looked at Ralph hoping he would answer. "We have prepared a funeral for him as soon as you're ready."

"So soon?"

"No time to wait, Victoria," Judy said. "There are a lot of his friends who want to pay their last respects before we leave."

Victoria sat up. "I'm ready. At least as ready as I'll ever be." She wiped her nose with the back of her hand and stood up off the cot.

Outside the militia commander was addressing his troops. She saw the same young girls from last week and marveled at their excitement. Only now they looked frightened as well, holding their rifles in front of themselves. The young men looked worried, too. *So young?* She wondered, *Was Orpine this young when he served in the Euro-Asia War?*

The commander spoke loudly. "We will need all our skills to survive this conflict," he said. "This is it--comrades--this is the real thing. No more practice. You must get it right the first time."

He looked from face to face at his young troops. "The bullets will be real and they'll be aimed at you. Don't take any needless risks. Remember to keep your eyes on the goal--the survival of the group."

Ralph stood next to the commander. The older man continued his speech. "There are hidden caches along the way. Each unit will have a map to where they are located. Use only what you need and leave the rest for the next unit. Ralph will be the guide for the first company."

Ralph nodded somberly.

Judy stood next to Victoria during the commander's address to his troops.

"Do they really think the government is going to attack?" Victoria asked.

"Yes," Judy answered.

"But this is going too far," Victoria said.

"Not when it comes to freedom," Judy said. "We have to fight for our freedom just like those before us. Someday others will realize what we've done and thank us."

"Judy, I've been back there. I've talked with those agents. They believe you're going to attack. This is dangerous. Anything could happen," Victoria said.

Edith stopped in front of the two women. She was carrying a heavy weapon strapped across her shoulder. Victoria thought it might be a rocket launcher.

"It is the End Times," she said.

Victoria studied Edith for a long moment. She wondered, *is this woman actually happy all this conflict is finally happening? Does she think it will prove something? Does she think it will prove she was correct?*

"It doesn't have to be the end of anything," Victoria said.

"The government is executing its plan to enslave us. It's too late to turn back now. Just as prophesied, many have ignored the warnings. Only a few are chosen. I feel sorry for all those who have been lulled into believing they are safe. Poor fools. The only protection is in the wilderness, in the Place of Safety where the Lord will provide for his chosen few just as He promised."

"Edith, it's not some universal, worldwide scheme to take away our freedoms. The government is trying to deal with real financial problems. You're making more out of it than it actually is."

Edith gave Victoria that you-unbeliever-look and fixed her jaw. "How can you say that after what's happened to you and your family? Of all people, I'd think you'd come to your senses and join our cause. How much more does the Lord have to test you?"

Victoria bristled. *How dare this woman try to imply my family's misfortune is some sort of test from God! Who does she think she is?*

Edith sensed she'd struck a nerve, as intended. She had no mercy for an unbeliever. "Anyone who isn't with us, must be against us," she said.

"That's not fair," Judy said. "We allow freedom, Edith, even when others don't believe as we do, even when they don't agree with us. Otherwise we're no better than the government we're resisting."

Edith grumbled and stomped off.

"I'm sorry," Judy said to Victoria after Edith left.

"She scares me," Victoria said, watching the woman leave.

Judy stood silently.

"Why is everyone leaving so soon?" Victoria asked. "If the authorities want anyone, it's me. They don't have any reason to come here, do they?" She wondered if something had happened that she wasn't aware of.

"Once the wheels start turning, there is no stopping. Now we have to stay the course," Judy said. "It's only a matter of time until they find us. Fortunately, we're well camouflaged here so they won't have an easy time locating us. Everyone will be dispersed before they arrive."

Ralph came back over to Judy and Victoria as the commander marched his troops further on. "It's time for the funeral," he said, taking Judy's hand.

The three walked silently to a private spot where several others were already gathered. Orpine's body was inside a roughly constructed pine box and wrapped in a dark green army blanket. The casket sat next to the recently excavated grave.

Victoria realized she would never see her husband again. The pain was nearly unbearable.

"Let us pray," the chaplain said, holding a small Bible in front of him.

Victoria stood between Ralph and Judy in case she needed their support. They seemed to sense this instinctively. At the close of the brief ceremony, Robin handed Victoria a small bouquet of wildflowers. Victoria smiled through her tears and thanked the little girl. She stepped forward as the casket was lowered into the ground and tossed the flowers onto it. She mouthed a silent "good- bye my love."

As people filed past her and offered condolences and hugs, Victoria felt a growing numbness and feared losing herself in the depths of grief. She hardly saw the faces of those who spoke to her.

"Victoria, can we do anything for you?" She looked at the man standing before her, David, Orpine's best friend. His eyelids were red and swollen, an odd thing, she thought, for a man to have cried so much.

Orpine and David had shared so much before she married Orpine, memories and horrors that he would never tell her about. Only those who participated could ever understand and she was grateful Orpine had such a friend. Perhaps this made David's grief so much greater, having lost someone that understood his own sufferings.

She tried to smile but failed. "I'll be okay," she said.

Joy held a bundle in her arms.

"Is this your new baby?" Victoria asked.

Joy nodded and hugged Victoria. The baby squirmed softly between the two women. Victoria could feel its tiny body and smell the newborn scent. So fresh, she thought. New life and the end of life, how ironic. Somehow it made her feel encouraged inside and put things into perspective. This little baby had all the potential in the world ahead of her. She hugged Joy a little harder and whispered, "Good luck, be careful."

"We will," Joy said. "Remember, we're here for you anytime you need us."

"You've got plenty to worry about. Forget me. I'll be just fine." She feigned bravery and forced a smile and took a little peek at the baby. "Is it a boy?"

"It's a girl," Joy said. "We named her Hope," David said. "For the New World, Hope."

"That's a nice name." She kissed the baby's tiny head and noticed Joy had dressed her in the clothes she'd given them the week before. She smiled at Joy.

They moved on and Victoria looked down for a moment, overcome momentarily as she remembered their offer to name their baby after Orpine if it was a boy. He had been so pleased by that. Undoubtedly they would have asked them to be the baby's godparents. *Would have,* she thought.

"I'm so sorry, Victoria."

She looked up at the sound of a familiar feminine voice. "Daria! When did you get back?"

"I came this morning."

The two women hugged. Daria was the one person who might understand how she was feeling having lost her own

246

husband so recently, and like Victoria, not being a true believer. Victoria felt an even greater common bond now.

"I thought you'd gone back to live with mainstream society. You never did like it out here in the wilderness."

"Yes. I did. I missed my friends," Daria said awkwardly. "Besides, I had some unfinished business."

"Where are your children? Didn't they come with you?" "No."

Victoria felt a twinge of panic. Daria never went anywhere without her children. She was the most protective mother Victoria had ever known.

Daria glanced around. "Victoria, you need to get out of here. I know you don't belong in this group any more than I did. These people are all crazy!"

Victoria thought for a moment trying to figure out exactly what her old friend was saying. "They aren't really crazy. They're sincere," she said. "I may not believe all their conspiracy nonsense, but I know they are sincere." She thought of Edith and added, "for the most part, anyway."

"Sincere or not, you don't belong here," Daria said sternly.

"Why did you come back, Daria? Why today?"

Daria looked guilty. "You have to leave Victoria. Come with me. I'm going back now." There was urgency in the tone of her voice, but before Victoria could pursue the matter she saw Jeremy running towards them.

"What's that?" he said, pointing away in the distance. Everyone listened. The sounds came closer and it became clear what it was. Helicopters.

Victoria glanced at Daria and knew what she'd done. "Oh my God, Daria! You've led them right to us. It's your S.I.N. They followed you here."

"What?" Ralph looked at Victoria, and then at Daria. "She's got an implant. It's her S.I.N. That's how they trace people. No one can hide and she has led them here," Victoria said.

Everyone started running as a large black helicopter swooped over the treetops. It was followed closely by two more helicopters.

Marelle grabbed Robin's hand and began running. Robin dropped her Rag Doll. Victoria and Jeremy followed Marelle and they all hid behind one of the earth house mounds. Victoria peeked around to see what was happening and Marelle peeked around on the other side.

Edith ran out from behind one of the houses holding her mobile rocket launcher.

Daria screamed from behind a large tree. "No! Don't shoot. They're not going to attack. They promised no one would be hurt."

It was too late. Edith took aim at the next helicopter that passed overhead and fired one of the rockets. It exploded and shrapnel flew in every direction.

Daria gasped and ran into the woods.

"We have to run," Victoria yelled to Marelle.

Victoria looked back around the hut. "Where's Robin?"

"She's right here," Marelle said, turning around. When she looked out into the open area she panicked. There was Robin running through the rubble to retrieve her Rag Doll. Marelle sprinted after her just as a large helicopter swooped down spraying automatic gunfire.

"Oh-my-God! NO! Marelle. Come back!"

Jeremy cried, "Mom!" and started after her.

Victoria grabbed him and held him back. "Let me go!" he cried, squirming to get away.

"Wait, Jeremy."

Marelle slumped to the ground. The helicopter flew away. Jeremy pulled away and ran out to his wounded mother.

Victoria darted out from behind the building and looked around for Robin. Dust rose like a noxious gas from the bullet sprayed ground.

There she was, clutching her Rag Doll in the middle of the confusion, crying for her mother. Victoria glanced over towards Marelle. Jeremy was helping her limp to safety.

Militia were setting up buffers with machine guns. Edith had taken cover behind a bunker and was reloading. Victoria saw another helicopter coming their way.

She sprinted towards Robin. Bullets splattered all around her as she dodged and weaved towards the little girl. She grabbed her in full run and dove behind a tree, shielding Robin with her own body. When she looked back, Jeremy and Marelle were gone.

"I want my Mommy," Robin cried, sucking her thumb and clinging to the doll.

"We'll find her, dear," Victoria said, examining Robin to make sure she was uninjured. They ran into the woods as several helicopters landed and began unloading heavily armed S.W.A.T. teams.

Two hours later, Victoria could still hear the distant gunfire as she caught up to some of the militia units. Most of the women had gone ahead to escort the elderly and children. Everyone wore camouflage outfits and was heavy laden with weapons and ammunition. Victoria wondered how they'd managed to stockpile so much.

The march was solemn and silent. Some of them sported bandages red with fresh blood. Some had dust-stained tear streams on their faces.

"Jeremy!" Robin cried releasing Victoria's hand and running towards her brother.

Victoria was relieved to see him and hurried over. "Where's your mother?"

"She's over there in the medic van," he said, pointing at a wagon-covered vehicle.

Victoria went over to the van. It stopped for a moment and Victoria climbed inside. There were several wounded people and a young woman tending to them. Victoria looked around and spotted Marelle. She glanced at the young woman who shook her head sadly.

Victoria climbed in beside Marelle. The young woman looked up a Victoria. "Is Robin all right?" she whispered.

"She's fine," Victoria said with a nod. "They're both fine. They are outside right now."

Marelle took Victoria's hand and looked into her eyes.

"Promise me you'll look after them" she said.

Victoria looked surprised. "Marelle, you're their mother. You'll look after them. I'll help you. Don't worry. Everything will be all right."

Marelle grimaced in pain. Tears streamed down her face. "Promise me, Victoria. You're the only one I trust. We're connected, remember?"

"I promise, Marelle. They'll be safe. Don't worry. Now rest."

As Victoria stood up to go, Marelle held her hand tightly. Victoria looked back down at her. "You were right," Marelle whispered.

"Right about what?"

"Reality isn't preordained. I shouldn't have said those things to you about your little girl. You didn't choose for her to die."

Victoria didn't know how to respond. "Don't worry about that now."

"No, Victoria. I was wrong. I didn't choose for this. I don't want my children to die. I don't want them to grow up without their mother," she choked. "This isn't a reality I chose."

"They haven't lost their mother. Don't talk like that. You'll be all right. Rest."

"Promise me you'll take care of them for me?"

Victoria nodded. "You know I will."

"I'll do the same for you," Marelle said. "On the other side. I'll take care of your little girl, too."

Victoria searched Marelle's face thoughtfully. "I know." She choked back tears and held Marelle's hand unable to speak further, her words stuck deep in her throat.

When they arrived at the fortified encampment deep in the Allagash woods several hours later, Victoria realized the militia had prepared well for this scenario. She got Robin and Jeremy safely inside one of the well-camouflaged earth houses. Edith entered shortly thereafter and spotted Victoria. "Come with me," she ordered.

"Where?" Victoria asked.

"We need every able-bodied adult," Edith said, exiting the house.

Victoria followed reluctantly. They went inside another bunker and when she came back outside, she was also dressed in Army fatigues and carried a weapon and belt full of ammunition. "You don't have to show me how to use it," she told Edith who was waiting for her. "Orpine taught me."

Mel ran into the camp. Scattered troops staggered in behind him. Victoria ran over to him. "How bad is it?"

"It's bad. We lost quite a few. The authorities are going to be coming soon."

"What about Daria?"

"Daria?"

"She was with me at the funeral when the helicopters came. Isn't she with you?"

"No. I haven't seen her."

"She led them to us," Victoria said. He looked at her in disbelief. The Commander and Ralph caught up to them just in time to hear her last statement.

"Who led them to us?" Ralph asked.

"Daria," Victoria answered.

Ralph sighed deeply with and expression of both grief and disappointment. "How could she do that?"

"It was her S.I.N.," Victoria explained. "It's also a tracking device."

"I knew we shouldn't trust her," Edit quipped. "She was one of them. All along, a Judas in our midst."

"If you hadn't fired, maybe they wouldn't have attacked," Victoria said, clenching her jaw.

"They were ready to attack. Didn't you see the guns aimed at us? If I hadn't shot that copter when I did, you'd be dead!"

"It's too late to second guess now," Ralph stated giving Edith a stern look.

"No one fires until given the order," the commander said. "Try to remember that next time. A good soldier follows orders."

Edith stomped away grumbling she only took orders from the Lord. Cappy followed after her.

"This is crazy," Victoria said to the group now gathered around them. "Don't you understand what's going on? The government won't stop until they win. Everyone will die."

Ralph glanced at Judy somberly.

Victoria looked from the commander back to Ralph. "You expect them to attack. They expect you to attack. Both sides are misunderstanding the other. This is a no-win situation."

"You better check your facts," the commander said shortly, "and read your Constitution."

"The fact is that both sides are afraid of the other. No one else needs to die," Victoria pleaded.

"What do you suggest?" Judy asked.

"We have no choice. We must fight," Ralph said. "The dominoes have started to fall and there's no turning back now," the commander said.

"None of us really wanted it to come down to this. We hoped they would just leave us alone. But they couldn't do that. We're too much of a threat to their power and their plan to enslave our country. We must fight. It's our God-given duty!"

"It's your fear that is destroying you, not some world- order conspiracy. Can't you see that? It's a self-fulfilling prophecy," Victoria argued.

"It doesn't matter now," Ralph said.

Victoria tried to reason once again. "The government thinks you're a threat when all you want is your freedom. They fear you just like you fear them," she said.

"Even if that's true, Victoria, it's too late now," Ralph said.

Judy nodded.

"What do we do now?" Mel asked.

"We've got to stop them," Ralph said.

"And get Trioxin," the Commander added. "We're going deep into the wilderness now and we'll be there for a long time. We need a big amount or we're going to lose a lot of Vets."

"I have an idea," Victoria said, surprising herself. They looked at her. She bit her lip. "I know exactly where to get it, but I'll need some help."

Chapter 14

Independence Day

An hour later, Mel and Victoria accompanied by two other soldiers, packed into an all-terrain vehicle, and headed out. They carried ammunition, explosives, and containers of extra fuel.

Robin ran over to the vehicle and took Victoria's hand. "Please don't go away," she said.

"I'll be back. Take care of your mom for me," Victoria said. She smiled and the child released her hand and waved to them as they drove off.

"Good Luck!" Ralph called.

As they traveled over the bumpy terrain, Victoria noticed the young female soldier sitting beside her. *She's so young*, she thought, *still wearing her hair in pigtails. And so somber*.

"Are you scared?" Victoria asked.

"Yes," the young woman nodded.

"Me, too."

It was almost 7:30 when Mel dropped Victoria off at the Veteran's Central Distribution Warehouse in Woodinville. "Give me two hours to create the distraction at the Government Processing Center at 9:30. That'll keep the authorities busy so you can steal the Trioxin," he said.

Victoria nodded. She knew the plan.

"You know how to use the explosives to open the door?"

She nodded again.

"I'll be back to pick you up at 22:00."

She looked at him remembering the last time when he said he'd wait for her.

"I promise," he said.

She waved and they drove off. Victoria headed towards the warehouse and hid in the shadows, waiting for the opportunity to get back inside.

What if they don't have a delivery tonight? She suddenly thought, *how will I get in?* She glanced at her watch. It was 7:30 PM. She waited an hour before the delivery truck arrived and began to unload his goods. The same guard helped as before.

Victoria edged closer, hiding behind the large truck. She watched them in the door mirror. When they went inside, she hurried up the ramp and stuck her toe into the door just before it latched shut. It pinched even with her army boots and she winced in pain.

She waited a moment, then gently pushed the door open just enough to slip inside. The hall was empty but she heard voices from the guard's office. She let the door latch slowly behind her hoping they wouldn't hear it. It clicked shut. She made her way down the hall towards the warehouse.

Victoria stopped in front of the door where she'd found the computers. It was only 9:00. She'd have to wait until Mel created the distraction at 9:30, so she slipped inside the room again. No sense risking the guard seeing her on his videos, or accidentally setting off an alarm.

It was dark inside the room except for the blinking green lights on the computer screens. She sat down in front of one and pushed a button. The screen lit up.

I wonder if I can get an outside line on this machine, she thought. She moved the mouse through several screens and finally located an icon for phone. She clicked twice and then through another menu until she was online with the Web.

She typed: SPIDER.

A moment passed as she nervously watched the doorway. Then a small screen inset appeared in the left- hand corner. A spider watched her while it moved in a computer-generated way. Its tiny eyes sparkled and she couldn't stop watching the animated creature.

She smiled. *Creative hacker*, she thought.

"You called?" the computer voice said a little too loudly, especially in such a quiet room.

Victoria glanced behind her to see if anyone approached. *How do I turn the sound down?* She fumbled with the switches in the back of the video screen, turned various buttons, some affecting the video quality. Finally, satisfied she'd at least lowered the volume, she typed: YOU'RE INSIDE.

There was a pause. *Just what I thought. All talk.*

"Inside?"

THAT'S WHAT I SAID. YOU'RE INSIDE

The spider moved about. *Cat got your tongue?* She smiled, wondering if this hacker really could do anything. That would create quite a distraction, she thought.

"Do you have the disk?"

She reached into her jacket pocket and pulled it out. She typed: YES

"Put it inside the drive."

WILL I BE DETECTED?

"Yes. After you execute the program they'll know where you are."

HOW MUCH TIME WILL I HAVE BEFORE THEY DETECT ME?

"Five minutes, tops."

I HAVE TO DO SOMETHING FIRST. CAN YOU WAIT?

"How long?"

She looked at her watch. It was 9:15. She typed: 20 MINUTES

"I'll wait."

She slipped the disk back into her pocket and went over to the door and listened. When she glanced back at the computer screen, the saver flicked back on and the screen went black except for the green blinking light again.

Victoria crept out into the hallway and made her way towards the storage room, suspecting silent alarms might already be triggered. She passed the surveillance room and peeked inside. The guard was sitting alone and watching a ball game on TV while drinking a cup of coffee. She assumed it was coffee. The deliveryman was gone. So far, so good.

She pulled out her 9-millimeter handgun and attached the silencer. She pushed open the door. "Put your hands in the air," she yelled.

The startled guard dropped his cup and stood up, holding his hands high. "Don't shoot."

He recognized her. "It's you! You came back."

"Turn around."

"Don't shoot me. I was only doing my job. Honest, it wasn't nothing personal. Please don't shoot me."

"Shut up and turn around. NOW!" She marveled how authoritarian her voice sounded considering her rapid heartbeat and quick breath.

He did. Beads of sweat formed on his brow. She secured his hands behind him and pushed him into the chair, sliding it back to the corner away from the equipment.

She took a roll of tape from a drawer and taped his mouth shut, all the while he was pleading with her not to shoot him. Then she taped his feet together and pushed the chair over so that he was lying on the floor. Satisfied he was no longer a threat, she searched for keys and found them. She checked the console. No sign of alarms. She left the room.

Victoria scanned the ceiling and walls for motion detectors. There were several and one started blinking red. It must have been tripped when she opened the doors to the main warehouse. She ran towards the small room in the back where she was sure they stored the Trioxin.

When she reached the door with the tiny window, she quickly tried each of the guard's keys. None of them fit. She reached inside her pack and located a small device. She attached it to the door, pushed a button, and hid behind a large shelf until the explosive went off. With a puff, the door opened. She glanced around quickly to see if she were still alone.

Victoria grabbed all the bottles of Trioxin stored inside the room and stuffed them into her oversized pockets and the pack she carried. She turned around. Lights were blinking everywhere. Even though she couldn't hear any alarms, she knew they'd gone off. Time was running out. Undoubtedly the police were already on their way.

She looked at her watch. It was 9:40. She hoped Mel had successfully done his diversion at the computer processing center. He would be back in 20 minutes.

She sprinted down the hall. A quick glance into the surveillance room and she could see the guard still on the floor. She ran into the small computer room and pushed the button. The screen came back on.

"Where were you? I was getting worried."

QUICK. HOW DO I EXECUTE THE PROGRAM?

"Insert the disk."

Victoria took the small rectangular disk out of her pocket again and pushed it back into the disk drive. NOW WHAT?

"Execute the program."

There was a pause and Victoria feared it was going to take too long. Where are the icons? I CAN'T USE A COMPUTER WITHOUT ICONS!

"Yes you can. This way they fill find it harder to stop the virus and locate you."

HURRY. I DON'T HAVE MUCH TIME

"Type exactly what I tell you."

OK

"Copy A:SIN"

She did. The computer copied a file named Do SIN

Now type DO SIN

She typed DO SIN and the computer began working. A few seconds later it asked for the date. She quickly entered 07/04/42

Victoria watched as formulas scrolled across the screen. *How long does this take*, she wondered? The spider in the corner moved about its box.

The computer stopped working. The screen read: Name of New tax?

WHAT DO I DO?

"Pick a name."

She thought for a moment and then typed: SIN TAX Victoria smiled.

"Good job," Spider said. "Now type SET LOOP."

She did and pressed the "enter" key. A form letter scrolled on the screen. She read it quickly as it rolled up the page. It said:

The good faith and credit of the United States Government is a lie. There is not faith. It is all credit. You are in debt and the government is broke. It's all an illusion. It's all a big lie. The day of reckoning has come. It's time to pay back all your debts. Today is your Independence Day. You are no longer dependent on the government!

"Wow," Victoria marveled. "Happy Independence Day, America!"

"Imagine what people will think when they read this on their computers," Spider said.

The computer paused as if waiting for another command.

WHAT DO I DO NOW? "

Type: NEXT"

She did.

Another message scrolled across the screen:

You have just been assessed your annual SIN Tax. The balance in your account is now ZERO. If you have any questions, send your inquiries in writing, on the proper forms and notarized, to the Bureau of Consumer Trade. They will respond according to the law. Please allow 30 working days for a reply. Have a nice day!

The computer paused again. Spider said, "RUN"

Victoria looked at the door. No one was coming. Run?

"RUN. You must start the program. RUN"

Run? She heard noises outside the building and glanced at her watch. It was 10PM. What do I do?

Sirens screeched outside and she heard the outside door opening. Boots pounded in the hallway.

"For God's sake, I'm a teacher, not a computer programmer!" she muttered.

"Type: RUN!"

Oh, she said, and typed RUN just as footsteps started coming down the hallway. The screen began scrolling the program and the spider disappeared.

Victoria ran to the door. The footsteps ran past her door. She peered out carefully and saw the police heading towards the storage room. Someone spotted the guard and yelled, "he's in here!"

She slipped out of the computer room and ran back to the loading door. Just as she got there, she saw dozens of police cars outside and pulled back out of sight.

Her heart was pounding. There must be another way out, she thought and ran back towards the monitoring station. She ducked into another hall just as the troops came back out of the warehouse. They were shouting. "She's got to be here! Seal the doors! Find her!"

She noticed a red EXIT sign and followed the arrows. The police were right behind her. She ran as fast as she could. The Trioxin bottles rattled in her pack. She burst out of the back door and sprinted into the alley. *Where are you Mel?*

She panicked, looking everywhere. The police were coming! The doors behind her burst open. She darted through the bushes to the next street.

There was Mel, waiting next to the all-terrain vehicle. The two young militia soldiers were standing guard. "Cutting it close," he said as they jumped inside and sped off.

A police car passed nearby. A single man was driving. Victoria looked at him and saw that it was Detective Henry O'Donnell. He looked straight ahead.

"I know that man," she said to Mel.

"Did he see you?"

"If he did, he isn't letting on. Hurry!"

Their vehicle was able to take paths others couldn't follow and they were soon far from the pursuing police who were searching the city and major highways.

As they passed through Phalarope Landing two hours later, Victoria asked Mel to stop at Warren and Val's farm. She wanted to thank them. When she knocked on the door, no one answered.

"They're probably asleep," Mel said. "It is midnight you know."

"No. Something is wrong. I can sense it," Victoria said as she headed for the barn. Warren's old truck was gone. She peeked inside the windows and gasped. "The house is ransacked," she told Mel. "Look."

He peeked inside, too, then went back to the front door and broke it down. They walked inside while the two militia soldiers kept guard at the vehicle. Furniture was overturned and dishes were broken on the floors. Every room was completely destroyed.

"What happened?" Mel asked.

"I think they were targeted because Warren tried to help me that day by using his S.I.N. to get Orpine's Trioxin," Victoria said.

"That's Warren. He was always sticking his nose into other people's business," Mel said.

"He and Val were helpful," Victoria said in Warren's defense. "I don't think it was meddlesome at all. I think it was sweet."

"What do you suppose they were looking for?" Mel asked.

"This isn't about looking for something," Victoria said. "This is hateful. They just destroyed everything without cause. Probably wanted to send a message."

Mel nodded. "I think you're right. Hateful. These poor old folks never hurt anyone."

"I hope they're all right. I hate to think I caused them so much trouble," Victoria said.

"Probably in a detention center," Mel said.

"Oh no!"

"It's not your fault, Victoria. It's the system."

"I will have to find them," she said.

"Later. We have to get back now."

They returned to the militia encampment just as the sun rose over the horizon. Ralph greeted them. "Did you get the Trioxin?" he asked anxiously.

Victoria pulled the jars from her pocket and handed him the backpack. "This should last a good long time," she said proudly.

Ralph smiled broadly and gave them a grateful, look, nodding. "Good job!"

"They're going to be busy for a while," Mel said with a grin.

How's that?" the Commander asked, now standing next to Ralph. "Did you create a bigger diversion?"

"Not me. Victoria gave them something else to think about besides us."

Victoria blushed. "Everyone will have something to think about when they go online, "she said. "I can't take the credit. I had some help."

Judy brought over coffee. "You must be exhausted," she said, handing them each a cup. The two soldiers on the back had slept most of the night and now headed into one of the earth houses.

"Great work, guys," Mel called after them. They only waved warily and continued into the house.

Victoria and Mel headed into the nearest earth house with Judy and Ralph. "Got some of your friends here," Ralph said.

"Who?" Victoria asked.

"Warren and Val."

"They're here?"

"Yep. They showed up a few hours after you left. Said they are on their way to visit relatives up north in New Brunswick."

Judy looked at Ralph. "I think they decided they'd had enough of the constraints and restraints of government." She grinned at her husband.

"Ralph and I plan to rebuild," she said. "Further into the wilderness, of course, when things calm down."

"It won't be the same, though," Ralph said. "We're not intending to be a store like before. Too hard to get stock. No, we just want to make a life for ourselves and do what we can to help others."

Judy leaned close to Ralph. "Maybe, someday, Coralee will understand," she whispered .

Victoria smiled. "How is Marelle?" she asked.

Judy sat her coffee cup down. "She died a few hours ago," she said. "I'm sorry. I know she was your friend."

"Where are her children?" Victoria asked.

"They're in there," Judy said, pointing outside towards a tent.

Victoria went to the tent. Robin was asleep with her Rag Doll in her arms and her faced stained with dried tears.

She looked over at Jeremy and noticed some movement. A dog whined. It was Delight!

Jeremy woke when Delight whined at Victoria. She was hugging the dog trying to calm her down. "Your dog sure does get excited," Jeremy said, rubbing his eyes.

"She's still a puppy," Victoria said, smiling. She took the dogs face in her hands. "Let me see you," she said tenderly, examining the dogs head. There was a bruise on her forehead and the dog whined when Victoria touched it. "Oh, that hurts, doesn't it girl. I'm sorry I had to hit you. I thought I'd killed you."

"Why'd you do that?" Jeremy asked.

"Because she was going to give us away. I had to protect you and your sister and your mother. You're more important than a dog." She looked at Delight. "Even though I love you," she said to the dog and hugged her.

Jeremy looked sad and Victoria sat down beside him. "I'm sorry about your mom," she said. He nodded quietly. She put her arms around him. "I made your mom a promise."

"What?"

"I promised her I would take care of you and your sister. Is that okay with you?"

He nodded and wiped a tear from his cheek. He reached into his pocket and pulled out the pink amulet. He handed it to Victoria. They hugged.

Delight whined and Victoria included her in the hug, too.

Epilogue

July, 50 years later

"What did you say your article was for?" Robin asked. "Sunday's edition to commemorate the 300th anniversary of the Fourth of July," the reporter answered.

"Why do you want to write about Victoria?"

"She made such a difference," the young woman answered. "People are still interested in her, even after all these years."

Jeremy scratched his graying beard. "There was complete chaos after the system went down," he said.

"People panicked," Robin added. "Everyone was afraid they wouldn't be able to buy food and stuff."

The young interviewer jotted some notes on her pad and looked up. "I researched the archives for news footage from that period. There were looters smashing store windows and stealing everything in sight."

"In the big cities people went crazy, starting fires and storming government buildings demanding their money," Jeremy said.

"It wasn't just the idea of a SIN Tax," Robin said. "It was the message that the good faith and credit of the United States Government was a lie. That there was no money, only an illusion. People suddenly thought they had no wealth, only debt."

"That's right," Jeremy said. "Once people realized the country was in debt, they lost confidence in the system and the whole monetary structure fell apart."

"People began bartering and used old gold and silver, whatever they could find."

"The great movement that the authorities had feared never happened," Jeremy said. "Most people were too addicted to the government programs to consider doing away with them completely."

"That's when Congress enacted the Financial Privacy Bill of Rights," Robin said.

"And Victoria went to Washington?" the reporter asked.

Robin handed her an old photograph. It was Victoria and Detective Henry O'Donnell on the front steps of Congress. "Victoria told us that she believed Henry left that disk there on his desk on purpose for her to find it. She thought he hoped all along something would happen because he'd seen many abuses of the system. He never would admit it, though."

"The Supreme Court banned the use of the implants," Jeremy said. "It was a violation of our civil rights."

"All that because of your mom?" the reporter said. "Victoria was our adopted mother," Jeremy said. "She would never take credit for all that. There were lots of other people involved, too."

"The Bureau of Consumer Trade was dismantled," the reporter said.

"Lots of indictments," Robin said.

"It put an end to the abuse of power," Jeremy said, "but not in time to save our biological mother. She was killed in the first battle."

"Weren't most of the defendants acquitted?" the interviewer asked.

"Yes," Jeremy answered. "Finding them not guilty only fueled the conspiracy believers. To this day some people still think there's a global plan to take over the country and enslave all of us."

Robin looked at the reporter thoughtfully. "Victoria said they were just over-zealous bureaucrats. She said most of them were probably sincere and believed they were doing the right thing but just got carried away."

"That's when the President pardoned the protestors?" the reporter asked.

Both Robin and Jeremy nodded. "That didn't set well with a lot of people," Jeremy said. "They thought someone should pay for the deaths of all those police."

"A lot of civilians died, too," Robin pointed out.

"You did get sent to reservations," the reporter said. "Some felt that was a prison sentence."

"Oh yes, they set aside wilderness places and called them reservations for those who wanted to live free, but most people found they didn't like it so much once they got there." Jeremy said.

"Too wild," Robin said. "It was a romantic notion but not too realistic for most people."

"But you and Victoria stayed?" the woman asked. "We were true wilderness survivors. Orpine and Victoria's cabin was burned down." She handed another photo to the reporter.

"Who's that man next to Victoria?" the reporter asked. "That's Mel. I don't know what happened to him," Jeremy said.

"I think he just disappeared soon after the system failed. Victoria seldom mentioned him, and she was always sad when we asked," Robin said.

Jeremy nodded. "He had some problems with drugs. Lots of Vets did."

"All that was left from the cabin was a guitar," Robin said, returning to the photo.

"And Yerba," Jeremy added.

"Yerba?" the woman asked.

"See that cat?" Jeremy pointed at the tiger cat curled up next to the woman.

"That's a descendant of Yerba. Kind of looks a little like him, too." Robin laughed.

"We learned to live off the land and to respect the land. To love Mother Earth," Robin said as she fondled the locket that had belonged to Victoria.

"During all those years, didn't you ever want to live in a town? Be around other people? Have the comforts that society offers?"

Jeremy smiled. "Our adopted mother and our little brother considered leaving a few times, especially when it was tough.

There was something that kept Victoria here and we weren't about to lose another mother."

"I remember the first time she told us to call her mom," Robin said.

"You were crying for our real mother. Victoria made a deal with us. She said, I tell you what, since I lost my little girl and you lost your mommy, how about I adopt you two and you adopt me?"

He turned to Robin. "Do you remember that?"

She nodded. "I worried that I'd forget my real mother but Victoria told us that our loved ones are always with us in our hearts and that no one can make them go away. She said our mom lived in us, in our genetic code somehow and if we tried real hard, we could feel her presence around us."

"She used to say our loved ones are talking to us in the wind, and touching us in the rain, and smiling at us in the sunlight, just to reassure us that they still love us," Jeremy said.

"She told us that our mother wouldn't mind if she took care of us in this life because she was taking care of Victoria's little girl on the other side."

The reporter wrote quickly. "Interesting," she said.

"Wise," Jeremy said.

"Victoria had a big heart with room for all of us. We made a deal to always be a family and we kept it."

"Was that her greatest lesson to you?"

Robin and Jeremy thought for a moment. Jeremy said, "Victoria taught us to trust our instincts and make our own decisions. She said we should never try to find answers somewhere else, but that God guides us here, inside."

Robin nodded. "She had a tremendous faith. I guess she'd learned from her own mistakes and her observations of others. She detested people who couldn't use their own minds to decide what to do in life."

"Tell me about her son," the reporter said.

"Orpine was born in April 2039. We call him Piney," Jeremy smiled.

"He's a true free spirit," Robin said.

"Like Victoria," Jeremy added.

"Teaches at the University in Orono?" the reporter asked.

"Yes. He's a professor of History, specializing in the late 20th century pop music," Jeremy said. "Quite a musician, too."

"He comes home often," Robin said. "Brings his grandchildren to enjoy the outdoors."

"You must miss Victoria?"

"She lived a long time," Robin said. "She was 80 when she died."

"Do you wonder if she'd have lived a longer life if she'd resided where regular healthcare is available?"

"Everything in nature dies at its appointed time," Jeremy said. "Man is the only being who resists this inevitable end."

"She left this world content and fulfilled and all without the aid of the government. How many people can say that?" Robin asked.

"She certainly was a folk hero," the woman said.

Both Robin and Jeremy smiled. "She didn't feel that way. People were fascinated with her. Called her the New American Pioneer," Robin said.

"She just wanted to live peacefully and naturally with as little intrusion from the government as possible," Jeremy added.

"I guess she succeeded," the reporter said.

The end

Other Novels

By

Mary Ellen Humphrey

Faith

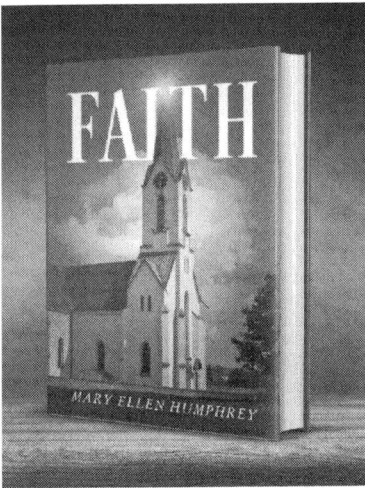

In the 1970's, three teenage girls become best friends when they are drawn into such a church, which promises hope, safety, love, and salvation. What they experience will challenge their faith in ways they never expected.

https://www.amazon.com/dp/0970717245

Norumbega

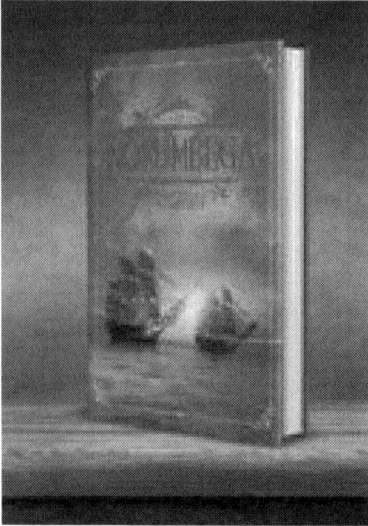

Leah Rigley disguised herself as a cabin boy in order to accompany her father, the captain of three ships, to the new world. She could not have anticipated the turn of events that would happen in the voyage and after the ships arrive at their destination. Travel with this extraordinary girl across the Atlantic Ocean in a 16th century sailing vessel and experience her adventures in the strange new world as she tries to find her way home.

"This is an exciting, well-crafted story of discovery and adventure set in 16th century New England...this tale has plenty of plot twists, actions, suspense, native lore and a surprise ending, as well as a young girl's learning about understanding, responsibility and love."

Kennebec Journal Review

https://www.amazon.com/dp/1074968875

Politics & Poltergeists

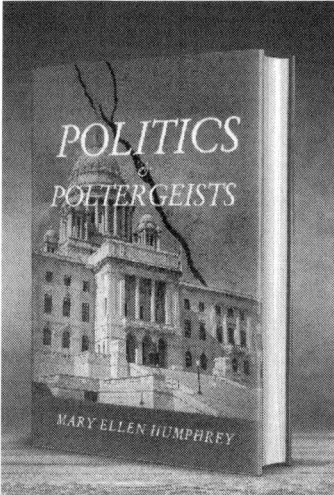

Could the State House really be haunted with the ghosts of politicians past? What would they say about how legislators work today? Travel the tumultuous political road with a politically challenged neophyte who must solve a real State House mystery.

https://www.amazon.com/dp/1692578146

The Last Right

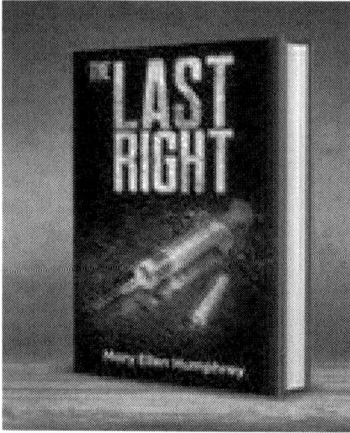

Jessica Willowby lives in the perfect world. Everyone is taken care of from cradle to grave. Issues like abortion and euthanasia have been solved, finally, in a fair and equitable way. Even criminals are treated for their disorders rather than sent to prisons. But at what price? Jessica finds out when her mother becomes terminally ill and she must fight the perfect system.

https://www.amazon.com/dp/1441426728

My Mountain Friend,

Wandering & Pondering Mr. Major

Part autobiographical, part memoir, all about finding oneself on a beautiful mountain trail in New Hampshire, this is the story of a "baby-boomer" searching for answers as she hikes, thinks, and discovers unexpected answers. All you have to do is ask, and then listen. This mountain has magic, age-old wisdom and maybe, even, love, for those who faithfully hike its trails.

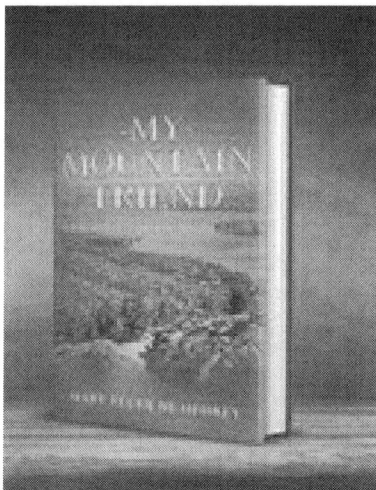

https://www.amazon.com/dp/B099WZG9V5

The Palimpsest Journal, Volume One

Carol Lynn, George, and Victoria

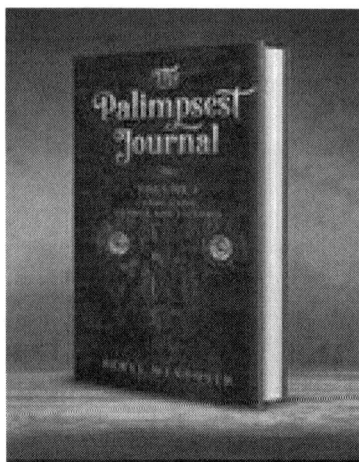

An ancient and mysterious journal changes the lives of those who write in it. The pages have been written over and over through centuries, yet to each new owner, the journal appears pristine and unused. Palimpsest refers to a very old text or document in which the writing has been removed, covered, or replaced by new writing. Ancient civilizations reuse writing surfaces like papyrus because paper was so valuable. In Volume One, meet three people who come into possession of a Palimpsest Journal: Carol Lynn, George, and Victoria. These are also available as individual mini ebooks.

https://www.amazon.com/dp/B09FS72STF

Made in the USA
Columbia, SC
25 June 2022